Delusions of Anubis

C. R. Turner

ISBN ePub 978-0-6483813-9-6
ISBN Mobi 978-0-6450800-0-1
ISBN Pbk 978-0-6450800-1-8
ISBN Hbk 978-0-6450800-2-5

I would like to thank the small team of people that has worked with me to create *Delusions of Anubis* – their expertise has helped bring it to life.

Thank you.

Emily Yau

Michele Perry

Nikki Bielinski

Bridget Bowe

Lenai Despins

Mike Nash

Cover Illustration by Mike Nash

w w w . m i k e - n a s h . c o m

Social Media

www.facebook.com/AuthorCRTurner

*For those who have fought their
demons in the darkest corner of
their mind and lost,
may your blessed soul find eternal
peace in the Kingdom of Osiris.*

Chapter 1

I grab my backpack and race out to the kitchen. Mom's looking beautiful, as always, wearing a black, knee-high skirt and blazer. She's clasping her necklace around her neck, the one she always wears with the feather of Maat amulet. Her golden Egyptian complexion, long, silky black hair and nice office clothes would make her standout in any crowd.

"What do you want for breakfast, Kyle?" she says as she spins around to look at me.

I'm standing next to the fireplace, hurriedly fitting my shoes. "I don't have time. I'll make you late."

"You have to eat something ... I'll make you some toast?"

I feel my stomach growl and relent to her offer. "Yeah, okay. Thank you."

Mom races about, whipping up my breakfast as I gather my books to stuff in my backpack.

"What time's your award ceremony tonight?" I ask.

"Seven thirty."

The toast pops, and Mom butters it for me before handing me the plate.

"Thank you. What's the Thomas Jefferson Award for again?" I ask while Mom wipes the benches down.

"It's for helping my students with their studies, mentoring them in my spare time. My work in helping the high school build their Middle Eastern language curriculum was cited as well."

"How many people will be there?"

"I don't know, I've never been to one here. In Cairo, some students and family members attend, as well as faculty members."

"Did you remind Dad?" I wonder if he'll even remember. *He'll probably be lost in his work, as usual.*

Mom makes brief eye contact with me and nods, but I sense a hint of reservation. It'll probably be just the two of us going tonight. It's a good thing I have my licence now, I can drive myself about instead of being let down by Dad and having to ask Mom all the time.

"Can I drive to school?" I already know the answer, but I have to ask.

"No!" she replies emphatically. "The roads are too slushy and icy. When you get more experience."

"But I have my licence now."

"I know, but you need more time on the roads. How about you come with me into Denver on the weekend, I have to go to the university. You can drive around the city by yourself? The streets are more regularly plowed and deiced than up here. It'll be safer."

I give an affirmative nod. "Okay, sounds good."

Mom has a joyous smile as she stands on her tiptoes to kiss me on the cheek. I think the reason she is so well liked has a lot to do with her bright outlook on life. I wish I could be more like her. We share a hug, and then I quickly wash my plate, still aware that I'm holding us both up.

As we walk out into the garage, I'm hit by the biting cold, and my breath mists the air. Dad's side of the garage is empty, as usual.

Mom climbs behind the wheel. I ride shotgun.

As Mom reverses out of the garage, I see a few inches of snow hiding the old, discolored shingle roof. Most of our twenty-acre property is white.

Mom's little four-wheel drive slushes through the mud and snow, and when we make it to the top of our long dirt driveway, she stops to redirect the heat to the fogging windscreen.

From part way up Colorado's Rocky Mountains, my hometown of Boulder is obscured under a white blanket, as well as the city of Denver in the distance. Blue Spruce and Douglas-fir branches bow under the weight of high-pitched roofs of snow. The sun burns with blinding intensity as it rises above the mountains in the distance – the promise of a new day.

"*Al hamdu Li Khepri, Ya ilahu al-Mashreq Al-Azeem,*" Mom says, smiling broadly.

"Praise to Khepri, O Great God of the east," I restate in English and grin back at her. Mom tends to revert to Arabic when giving her Egyptian praises.

Mom pulls out of the driveway, just as a huge semi – thirteen feet high of chrome and steel and plastic – barrels down the road, closing in at a terrifying rate.

My heart skips a beat. "MOM," I yell.

By the time Mom sees it, its tires are hollering, and its trailer begins to slide sideways.

Time slows to a crawl.

I gasp. My heart thunders.

Thirty plus tonnes of steel on a slush-covered country road hurtle toward us, unable to stop.

The driver's face forms a picture of pure fear.

Mom screams.

Still moving at considerable speed, the semi slams into the side of Mom's four-wheel drive.

A deathly cacophony of steel crumpling, glass exploding, and tires screeching blasts my ears. As the semi hits the driver's side, Mom's body is slammed against the changing shape of the driver's door. I wrench my eyes shut and I'm showered in glass. My seat belt tears at me as we're bulldozed down the road. My head strikes something hard, and darkness falls over me.

Red and blue lights flash against my eyelids as I regain consciousness. I open my eyes and feel my throat tighten; I'm about to retch. *What the hell just happened?* The smell of diesel wafts through the icy air. I look to my side where I see Mom lying motionless, lacerations all over her face and blood running down her cheek.

"Sir, can you hear me?" a man's voice calls out.

Where is he? I turn my head to see a man in black clothing with bright yellow stripes trying to open my door. His jacket has the local fire department's badge on it.

"Sir, can you hear me?" he calls again.

"Yeah," I reply, coughing.

"He's alert and responsive. Let's pop the doors," he calls out. "What's your name, sir?"

"Kyle," I reply. "Help my mom, she's not moving."

Why hasn't she come to yet? My guts churn with worry.

The firefighter pries my door open to the sound of steel creaking.

"Help my mom," I try to say, but the words don't quite make it out.

"The other firefighters are helping her. Just take it easy," he replies. "Stay where you are."

I remove my seat belt and swing my feet out onto the slush-covered road.

"Sir, you need to sit still. We need to fit you with a C-collar."

I stand on my shaky legs. "I'm okay."

He places my arm over his shoulder, taking some of my weight, as we shuffle over to the firetruck. "I'm going to put you down ... you ready?"

"Yeah." I gasp as he places me down on the firetruck's step.

"Wait here," he says before running back to the wreckage.

Mom's car has been pulverized. Every single window is smashed or cracked, and parts hang off it everywhere. The passenger's side tires are both flat and have been torn from their rims. *God, I hope Mom's okay.* I grimace as waves of nausea keep coming at me, and I swallow, trying hard not to retch. There are the sounds of firefighters yelling, some hydraulic whirring, and sirens in the distance.

I sit like this, taking in the chaotic sounds around me, until I hear an ambulance and police car pull up. One paramedic runs toward me while the other assists the firefighters.

"Sir, can you hear me? What's your name?" the paramedic asks, his rapid breath misting the air.

"Kyle."

"Do you know where you are?"

I struggle to my feet. "No ... wait." I stare at a letterbox nearby until it comes to me that it's ours. "That's my home."

"Can you walk? I can get the wheelchair or gurney."

"I'm okay. I can walk," I assure him.

He places my arm over his shoulder and helps me to the ambulance.

I look back. "My mom, we need—"

"The firefighters will get her out. She's in excellent hands."

Feeling faint, and with help from the paramedic, I make it to the ambulance just in time to collapse on the back step.

"We need to get you inside the ambulance, Kyle. Do you think you can climb up onto the gurney?"

I nod. My head throbs.

More sirens wail in the distance. It gives me hope. I collapse on the gurney. When the wailing stops, heavy doors slam and there's muffled yelling outside. The paramedic wraps me in a white blanket and fits me with an oxygen mask.

I'm so tired, all I want to do is sleep.

The paramedic measures my blood pressure. "Kyle, do you have any nausea or a headache?"

I nod weakly, holding back tears and a whole torrent of emotions. "I have a splitting headache; the left side of my head is killing me, and I keep getting waves of nausea."

Another paramedic climbs into the ambulance and looks me up and down. "Who's this? Is he a bystander?"

The paramedic treating me looks back at him. "He was in the four-wheel drive."

"What? There's not a scratch on him."

The other paramedic climbs into the front, and a second later, the heavy diesel engine shakes the ambulance as it starts.

"My mom ... is she okay?"

"The firefighters have her out ... just rest. If you need to sleep, you can."

I wake to the gurney bumping as it's rolled out of the back of the ambulance. The air is icy. Passing cars slush through the snow. The paramedics wheel me inside, and I'm hit by the clinical smell and chaotic atmosphere. Lights whisk overhead. A doctor appears by my side. As the paramedic is briefing him, a heavy frown sets upon his face.

"Kyle, my name is Doctor Mathews. How do you feel?"

"Nauseous."

He takes my oxygen mask off. "Do you have pain anywhere?"

"Mostly bad nausea and a headache."

Still frowning, he shakes his head ever so slightly. "Can you tell me your full name and address?"

"Kyle Roberts, seventeen thirty-one Conifer Crescent," I reply and then ask, "how's my mom?"

"She hasn't come in yet."

Doctor Mathews signals to one of the paramedics who pushes me through to a free space in the emergency department. I'm sat up and transferred to a hospital bed. I thank the paramedics for their help as they leave with their gurney. A nurse closes the curtains and helps me out of my clothes. As I take my jacket and shirt off, I fully realize what the paramedic had said: I don't have a scratch on me. I run my hands over my face but can't feel any bumps or lacerations.

How the hell is that possible?

The nurse helps me lie down on the bed, now in a hospital gown. She sticks little white plastic squares to my chest and then clips electrical cords to them. The machines beside my bed light up when she turns them on.

Doctor Mathews watches the screens for a short while and then runs his hand over my stomach. "Any abdominal pains?"

I shake my head.

"Any chest pains?"

"No."

After a brief examination, he shakes his head, deep in thought. "All right ... the nurse will take you to get a CT scan of your head and chest, okay?"

I nod.

I'm trying to picture what Dad's face will look like when he gets the news. I wonder if the accident will be enough to drag him away from work. Everything he does revolves around his stupid brickworks. His love for Mom is unquestionable, but I've often wondered if he cares about me.

My head is aching, and jumbled thoughts are coming at me in assaults. I shut my eyes and try to clear my mind.

The nurse helps me into a wheelchair and places my clothes, which are in a plastic bag, in my lap. She wheels me further into the hospital and soon we're outside a room with an enormous machine in the middle. Above the door, a back-lit yellow sign says: Controlled Area – X-rays.

My nerves build as I look the machine over.

What are they going to find?

The nurse enters the room and returns with a bottle of water. "Here you go, Kyle," she says, "you need to drink this before your scan."

I reply with a faint nod, trying not to shake my head to avoid the pain.

She hands me a clipboard with paperwork on it. "Can you fill this in, please? Do you have any allergies?"

I look up and shake my head.

I sit by myself, filling in the paperwork and taking sips from the bottle of water. My stomach is tying itself in knots. I have a million thoughts crashing around in my head.

When I finish, the nurse returns. "Can you stand?"

I nod and struggle to my feet.

"Are you okay," she asks again.

"Yeah ... I'm good."

A thin lady who looks to be in her fifties joins us inside the room.

"Hi, Kyle, I'm Mary. I'm your radiographer," she says, smiling. "Can you take a seat over here, please?"

I sit on a chair with padded armrests. They are the same chairs they use when giving blood, which gives me some comfort.

"I'm just going to insert a cannula into your arm so we can inject a dye for your scan, okay?"

"Okay," I reply, my nerves building at the sight of her tray covered in medical equipment.

"You'll be fine," Mary comforts me. "You'll probably get a metallic taste from the dye."

Once she inserts the cannula and tapes it in place, she attaches a short line and connects a syringe. I look away as she makes the injection.

"All over. You need to sit for a short while before your scan. I'll come back in a bit."

I nod. My nerves build with every passing second. Every shallow breath is hard work. I slouch against the back of the chair, feeling like I'm about to faint. The whole world seems to disappear into oblivion as I struggle to stay conscious. I flop my head back against the chair, shut my eyes and lay like this for a while, focusing on my breathing.

What feels like half an hour passes before I hear footsteps and lift my head.

"Are you okay?" Mary asks. "You're sweating bullets."

"I feel faint."

She makes a sympathetic face. "Do you think you can stand?"

Not sure, I struggle to my feet. She holds my arm and leads me over to the machine. I lie down, feeling the cold surface of the machine beneath me. I see two technicians working in a room off to the side behind glass. I tuck my gown in self-consciously to cover my legs.

"Lie as still as possible. The scan will take a couple of minutes, okay?"

"Okay," I reply, feeling my heart thumping in my ears.

It's quiet until a faint ubiquitous hum floods the room. A feeling of being completely powerless grips me. I swallow hard and try to calm my nerves.

After my CT scan, the nurse pushes me through the halls in the wheelchair. We pass a cafeteria, a small giftshop with get well cards and balloons, and dozens of rooms with patients in beds with the sounds of televisions escaping into the hallways. The hospital is huge. A couple of minutes later we reach a room, which holds just two beds, both empty. The nurse places my bag of clothes in the drawer of the nightstand. She pulls back the sheets and helps me up onto one of the beds. I plonk myself down on the edge just as Doctor Mathews walks in, holding a folder filled with papers.

"Do I have to stay?" I ask.

He looks up from his papers and says, "Just overnight for observation. Your CT scan looks good; there's no intracranial bleeding or abdominal injury. You're a lucky man to walk away from an accident like that without a scratch."

"What about my mom? When can I see her?"

He places his hand on my shoulder, and his face hardens.

My heart skips a beat.

He gives me a grave look, and I shudder. *No. Don't say it.*

"I'm sorry, Kyle, but your mom died at the scene. There wasn't anything they could do for her. I'm sorry."

It feels like all the oxygen has been sucked out of the room. I stop breathing as my heart drops like a bag of rocks. Tears stream down my cheeks. I begin to hit myself on the forehead over and over with my palm as inconsolable grief tears me apart. My brain scrambles.

I should have died with her.

Feeling dizzy, I remind myself to breathe, and I gasp hard.

My deepest fears have come true.

This can't be. There must be some mistake.

The nurse's face has transformed into one of sorrow as she stands by my bed, still holding my wrist after stopping me from hitting myself.

"Are you sure?" I ask quietly, almost not wanting to know the answer.

"Yes, we're sure," Doctor Mathews says. "I'm sorry, Kyle. Your father is on his way. We'll bring him straight in when he gets here."

Before I know it, Doctor Mathews has left. The nurse is close to tears as she brings me more pillows and some water. My head hits the pillows, and I picture Mom's face.

This isn't real. It can't be. I'll wake up soon and this will all be a horrible dream.

I grasp my forehead, close my eyes, and try to will all these dark thoughts from my mind.

I hear footsteps and open my eyes. Dad is standing by the side of my bed, his eyes bloodshot. He looks lost for words – more so than usual. His chin quivers. I wonder if today will bring us closer, or just divide us even further. The longer he stands there, my desire for him to hug me is replaced with disappointment.

"I'm sorry," I say.

"What for?"

"I should have driven. Maybe—"

"Don't be stupid," he cuts me off. "Don't think like that. It's not *your* fault." He reaches out and touches the edge of my bed as though unsure what to do. "So, how are you doing? Where's your head right now?" Dad asks softly, his tone suddenly changing.

I know he's referring to my "depression", which he hasn't asked about in years – and I wonder where this conversation might go. I look away and shake my head, not wanting to talk about it; now isn't the time – in fact there never is a time to talk about it.

When Doctor Mathews walks in, I recall the brutal reality of what has just happened and his last words to me, although I'm also relieved that his presence has killed the conversation about my depression – some old memories are better off remaining buried.

"Mr. Roberts, your son is very lucky. He doesn't have any injuries. I'd like him to stay overnight just for observation, though."

I wish he'd stop calling me "lucky." If I was lucky, Mom would still be alive.

"How is that possible?" Dad asks.

Doctor Mathews shakes his head. "These things happen from time to time."

The image of Mom, lying motionless, covered in blood, comes to my mind. I still can't believe she's gone. A tear races down my face, and I quickly wipe it away.

"I'll call you in the morning to let you know when you can pick Kyle up," Doctor Mathews says.

Dad nods, glances at his watch, and then stares at the wall in thought. I can just imagine what he's doing: rearranging his schedule in his head. Everything revolves around him and his stupid brickworks. I'm pissed off at him. *Why can't he take a break from his usual self-absorbed self for once?* I look out the windows at the snowy mountain vista to the west and try in vain to not shake my head.

"Can I speak to you a minute?" Dad asks Doctor Mathews, and the two of them leave the room.

I can hear them outside talking about me, about our time in Egypt and my depression. Doctor Mathews asks if I'm on antidepressants, and there's a silence, but I imagine Dad is shaking his head. I don't need to take medication. There's nothing wrong with me.

When Dad walks back in, he stands beside my bed. I can see him out of the corner of my eye, standing still, unsure what to say or do. I wish I could just have a normal dad; for us to be close. Now Mom's gone, I don't have anyone.

"Kyle," he says.

"What?" I reply, my anger rising.

"I know things haven't been good between us lately, but I want to be there for you."

"If you wanted to be a real father, you'd sell your damn company," I bark. "If you had been there ... if *you* had been driving ... maybe this wouldn't have happened." I almost regret letting him have it when I see his face contort in a mix of emotions: anger, sorrow, and ... something else – I'm not sure what. I shake my head and look away. Mom would have expected more from me.

"I'm sorry," I say and bury my face into my palms.

Dad sits on the edge of my bed.

What feels like a good half-hour goes by with neither of us speaking. To Dad's credit, he doesn't look at his watch once, and I feel even worse for barking at him.

"You can go if you want," I say.

He looks up, his face strained. "I'm not going back to work. Not now. They can handle things for few days without me."

Exhausted, I lie back and rest my head on the pile of pillows.

A thin crescent of the sun is all that remains above the mountains by the time I finish reading the fishing magazines Dad bought from the hospital's shop. Neither of us have fished a day in our lives, but I guess even Dad wouldn't be so insensitive as to buy car magazines right now. As he left, he said he'd "swing by work" before picking me up in the morning, which in the past could mean anything from a few hours to the entire day.

I wonder if he'll even give me another thought while he "goes back to normal."

In a couple of hours, Mom's award ceremony will be starting. We would have been at the university just down the road. I think back to this morning, remembering how Mom praised Khepri, God of the Morning Sun, as she did from time to time. I look at the remains of the sun out of the window and think of how the Sun God, Ra, is about to die in the west once again, after journeying through the sky. An endless cycle of life, death, and rebirth.

I'll never forget sitting in bed at night listening to Mom recite legends of the ancient Egyptian gods and pharaohs. Even though she had to stop and translate Arabic to English from time to time, I was always transfixed by her stories, and I looked forward to them each evening with excitement.

Now, sitting in bed all alone, my heart's in agony knowing I'll never see her again. I lie back, feeling depressed and absolutely exhausted, and shut my eyes to try to get some sleep. It's not long until the darkness of sleep finds me, and I drift off ...

Standing in a desert, which is carved in two by a great river, I glance around. There are no trees, no people, nothing as far as the eye can see. My heart pounds in my ears. Where am I?

Is this the Underworld, the Duat?

Am I dead?

The sky is black, and a darkness I've never seen before permeates everything. I walk through the thick darkness, searching for something, anything. There's a silence over the land, as though sound has been smote from existence.

Ahead, an inverted pyramidal frame hangs in the air. With no point of reference, I have no idea how far away, or how large it is. By my stride and the rate at which it appears to grow in size, it can't be too far away. Other than the desert and the river, it's the only thing in sight. What is it? A mirror? Then I realize: that's a portal.

Standing in front of the strange doorway, I stare into its darkness. Its frame is made of onyx and decorated with gold. Standing roughly five feet tall and hovering in the air, it paralyses me with fear, but at the same time I have an overpowering urge to touch it.

I find the courage to reach out and touch its deathly black surface. When my fingers make contact, a chill runs up my arm and floods my body. I try to pull away but can't. It's like my hand is glued to the portal's surface.

What little light there is dies. The desert and river vanish, and I'm suddenly surrounded by nothingness; only the portal remains, now reflecting a blueish

hue instead of blackness. My heart
hammers in my chest.

Now where am I?

I'm finally able to pull my hand away
and step back. My head spins as I
search for anything to cast my eyes on,
but other than the portal, there's
nothing to see: no sky, no ground, no
light. My breathing quickens, and my
heart races wildly.

I jolt awake and sit up in bed, my heart still
hammering in my chest.

What the hell was that?

The sun has set, and there's just a small amount of
light entering the room from the hall. I struggle to slow
my beating heart as I gasp for breath, but even a couple of
minutes later my heart still hasn't settled. I've never had a
nightmare feel so vivid – it almost felt real.

I rest my elbow on my knee and bury my face into my
palm, feeling completely alone. A tear streaks down my
cheek and drops onto the bedsheets. I can't imagine the
nightmare was real, but from everything Mom taught me

about ancient Egyptian mythology, who knows, maybe it was. Or maybe I'm just losing it.

Chapter 2

Outside, it's snowing lightly as I carry my discharge
papers to the carpark. The faded black paint of Dad's old
pickup truck stands out in the snow. He's had it for over
twenty years, and I guess he's kept it all this time to
remind himself of his humble beginnings as a bricklayer.
It's one of his few traits that I actually like – that he
doesn't buy needless crap.

I gingerly climb in – my head is still tender – and pull
on the door handle. With its airtight seal lost a decade
ago, the door crashes shut, and I cringe at the metal-on-
metal sound, which sends my mind back to the moment
of the collision. I grimace.

Dad climbs in, and a second later, the old engine
rumbles to life. One flick of the wipers sends the fresh
powdering of snow flying.

Dad drives over to the exit of the hospital carpark,
indicates and looks both ways. He barely touches the
throttle, but the crude vee-eight still spins its wheels

slightly in the snow, making my heart jump. I turn the heat up as the wind whistles through the gaps in the doors.

"Are you all right?" Dad asks.

A split second of eye contact. I swallow hard and nod.

We head along the dual-carriageway that bypasses Boulder before turning off and heading up the country road toward home. When I realize we will have to drive over the patch of road where Mom died, I take a rattled inhale of breath, my heart heavy with dread. I feel like I'm about to burst into tears and look out the side window as we pass, focusing on the snow-covered trees instead.

Dad's truck trundles down our dirt driveway, and our old house comes into view. Memories of playing with Mom outside in summer come flooding back, and I have to try with all my might not cry. I don't want to be here. The pain is too raw.

When the garage door opens, I stare at the empty spot where she would park her little four-wheel drive. I can understand why they call it heartbroken; this is debilitating, excruciating. Struggling to hold back my tears, I wait for Dad to open the door to the house, staring at the dusty concrete floor to avoid any eye contact with him.

I go straight to my room and close the door behind me. Resting my forehead against the wall, I feel a tear streak down my cheek. I draw a deep breath and exhale; a slight whimper escapes with it. Seeing my bookshelves, filled with books on ancient Egyptian mythology, makes my heart break even more, and a feeling of sorrow – that leads to depression – rages wildly.

I crash on my bed and wipe my eyes, feeling completely alone and wanting out of this reality.

A few hours later, I'm getting hungry. I can hear Dad in the kitchen and decide to see what he's doing. I check my eyes in the mirror. They're not too bloodshot.

"I'm going into Boulder to pick out a casket ..." he says as I enter. "Did you want to come?"

My heart flares in pain, and I lock up, unable to respond.

"I thought I'd get a pizza for lunch. Is there anything you wanted while I'm in town?"

Other than his red eyes, you wouldn't even know he was hurting. His steely eyes and emotionless mask-like face are the same as ever. He always looks like he's ready to kick the whole world's ass – not just his appearance, but how he carries himself – and there's no difference now.

I shake my head. Typical, back to microwave dinners and takeaway. I now regret not asking Mom to teach me how to cook for myself.

"Can I have Mom's feather of Maat amulet?" I have a feeling I already know the answer, but I ask anyway.

"You want to wear a necklace?"

"My *mom's* necklace," I counter, the rage rising within.

He stands there quietly, his disapproval subtly creeping over his features.

What's wrong with wanting a keepsake of my mom? I can't believe he could be so heartless.

"Forget I even asked," I yell, before storming off to my room and slamming the door behind me. Sorrow builds inside me until I burst into tears. I bury my face in my hands and tears stream down my cheeks.

When I hear Dad leave, I compose myself and go to have a shower, but as I take off my shirt and catch myself in the mirror, I stop. I'm still covered in the little white plastic sensors that were hooked up to the machines at the hospital. I rip them off, grimacing, and throw them in the trash. My body's aching, and I'm exhausted after hardly sleeping. I look at my pale complexion and unruly wavy hair and wish that I looked like Mom. She was so beautiful and kind.

Lying on the couch with a blanket over me, I'm just starting to doze off when the sound of Dad's truck wakes me. My stomach rumbles with hunger as I sit up. I stare at the clock a short while, thinking through my daze: three o'clock. He's been gone for hours. *Typical.* He probably stopped at the brickworks on the way home.

I meet him in the kitchen where he drops two pizza boxes on the bench.

"What took so long?" I don't bother hiding my anger. *He better not feed me some crap about an emergency at work.*

He reads my face and replies somewhat tenderly, "I went into Denver to order a heart scarab. I had to go to several shops before I could find one that could order it."

I look away. "Oh ... sorry."

Damn. I feel guilty for giving him attitude now. Mom would be grateful. She would have wanted to be buried with a heart scarab, an Egyptian amulet – a scarab beetle often carved in green jasper – which is worn around the neck for use in the afterlife, in case something happens to the deceased's own heart.

"When's the funeral?" I add, my voice breaking at the end of my sentence.

"Thursday," Dad replies.

I want to ask about Mom's feather of Maat amulet again, but it's probably pointless, so I sit quietly and eat the pizza. I glance up at Dad from time to time, but he seems to be avoiding eye contact as much as me, and he soon finds an excuse to leave the room.

After lunch, I return to my bedroom, and I'm surprised to see Mom's feather of Maat amulet sitting on my pillow. I gasp, my jaw dropping open. Dad can be a real ass, but now and then, he does do something from the heart. I pick it up and smile. It's made of dark brown leather from which a one-inch-long gold feather hangs. I run my thumb over the feather before putting it on.

Sitting on the edge of the bed, I pick up the hinged photo frame from my nightstand. Inside are two photos. On one side, an old, faded photo of my birth mom and on the other, a photo of me and Mom. The sight of Mom devastates me. My eyes well up, and I clasp her amulet. I can't believe how much this hurts.

I look to the other photo, running my fingers down the glass, and wonder what my birth mom was like. It's hard to miss someone you never even had a chance to meet, but the pain is still there.

I think back to the nightmare I had in the hospital. It had felt so real; it was like I was in the Duat for a brief moment. I wonder what it meant. Maybe I can find some answers in my book on The Ennead. I search through my shelves, looking through the selection of ancient Egyptian mythology books until I find it. Sitting up in bed, I glance at my clock radio. It's approaching bedtime. Dread rises from the pit of my stomach when I think about going to sleep. I hope I don't have any more nightmares.

It's the day of the funeral, and I'm getting dressed in the one suit that I own. I walk into the bathroom to see how I look and find that Dad's already in there, brushing back his hair. Like me, he's in his only suit. Our eyes briefly meet in the mirror's reflection. A thin smile appears on my face. Now both dressed the same, I can see how we look so much alike. We both have long wavy hair, strong jaw lines, blue eyes, and are both tall.

He takes my tie from me and wraps it around my neck, taking a lot of care and precision as he ties it for me. Once he's finished, he straightens it and studies me closely. The corner of his mouth lifts in a small smile before he walks out.

I pull Mom's feather of Maat out of my pocket and put it around my neck; the gold amulet's striking against my black clothing. Contemplating whether or not to tuck it in, I decide to leave it out. I look at myself in the mirror. Not bad for a mountain kid.

When we reach the end of the driveway, I search the road for any skid marks from the accident, but the snow is making it hard to even see the lines. I let go of the breath I didn't even realize I was holding in. Dad pulls out cautiously. I thought the first time we'd leave our driveway again would make me a nervous wreck, but all I can think about it seeing Mom's casket.

We drive through Boulder and pull into the cemetery. I can't imagine what's going through Dad's mind right now. He never shows much in the way of emotions, but I'm guessing he's heartbroken. How could he not be? This will be his second wife he's burying here.

"Did the heart scarab arrive in time?" I ask.

Dad nods.

"What's it made from? Green jasper?"

"Yeah. They ordered it in from Egypt."

I widen my eyes in surprise. "How did it get here so fast?"

"I had it air-freighted."

"It's on her chest?"

Dad nods, almost as if he's sparing me the details. I smile inwardly, picturing the scarab beetle carved in the green gemstone.

As we get closer, I notice a really long line of cars. There must be a couple of funerals on today, but when Dad pulls up, I realize the people are all here for Mom. *Why are there so many people?* There has to be at least fifty. *Who are they?* Most of them are in their early twenties, standing in small clusters.

Then it hits me. They must be Mom's university students. I can imagine how she must have touched so many lives – the beautiful soul that she was.

I see my uncle's red '72 Mustang a few spaces up, and then I spot him walking toward us. I had thought about buying his Mustang when I overheard him telling Dad he was planning on selling it. Now that the car is twenty years old, I don't think he'd want too much for it. Having just turned seventeen and gotten my licence, I had been excited about buying a car and hitting the open road by myself for the first time. I can't imagine doing that now. I don't even know how I'm going to move on with my life.

As I climb out, the snow crunches beneath my feet and a faint, ghostly howl blows through the trees. With the sky a light gray, and it not much above freezing, I do up the top button of my suit jacket to stay warm.

Uncle Tim shakes Dad's hand then pulls him into a hug. I can see it makes Dad uncomfortable. You'd think he'd be a little more affectionate toward his own brother, but then again, I know better than most how distant he can be.

My uncle turns to me and hugs me tight. "Kyle."

I walk by my uncle's side, feeling uncomfortable that so many people are looking at us.

A bald man and a woman in her early twenties break off from a group and approach us. The woman is holding something tight to her chest.

"Mr. Roberts," the older man says. "We haven't met, but I'm Professor Landstrom, I—"

"Oh, right. I know who you are," Dad replies. "Well ... I know the name."

"I'm so sorry for your loss," the professor says with a solemn face.

Dad returns his words with a nod, his expression of gratitude, although if you didn't know Dad that well, the sentiment may be missed.

"This is Penelope Smith," the man continues, gesturing toward the young woman.

"Mr. Roberts, I'm so sorry. Your wife was such an amazing woman," she says. "I was failing my Middle Eastern language studies and was on the cusp of dropping out when she took over our classes and started mentoring me. It was because of her I graduated last year. I was supposed to present her with the Thomas Jefferson Award at the ceremony the other night." She unfolds her arms and holds out the framed certificate.

Dad takes it, studying it for a short while. "Thank you," Dad says. "We appreciate it."

Professor Landstrom and Penelope return to their group, and Dad hands me the award as we make our way over to the priest. I've been dreading this moment, and when Mom's coffin comes into view, my heart shatters. I'm determined not to cry. I'll save that for when I'm alone.

Dad greets the priest, and Uncle Tim and I take a seat at the front.

Mom's coffin is a dark timber with a high-gloss finish and silver handles on the sides. It sits on straps that are connected to shiny stainless-steel bars that run down both sides to lower it into the ground. The hole beneath it is black, and it makes me think of the Duat, as though the dark hole is connected to the Underworld. Around the hole, artificial turf has been laid. Most of the snow in the immediate area has been shoveled away.

Dad takes his seat next to me, and the priest begins to speak. He talks about God and heaven, which feels kind of inappropriate when Mom was such a strong believer in ancient Egyptian mythology. There was no heaven or hell in ancient Egypt, just the Duat where the soul goes to be judged, and if judged favorably, the soul lives in peace for eternity. For the most divine, they could leave the Duat and live with the gods in the celestial sphere as an imperishable star.

I pull a golden eagle feather and shabti from my pocket. The feather has sat on my bookshelf for the past year. I fondly remember Mom and me seeing it in a shopfront in Denver and going in to buy it. There was a wave of understanding between us that day, that the feather symbolized the blending of our two cultures: the feather of Maat from her Egyptian heritage, and the

Golden Eagle from my American heritage. The shabti, which took me nearly all day to carve from a block of wood I found around the house, stands about six inches tall, and it looks pretty good, if I do say so myself. It even resembles Mom with her long hair, and its small size reminds me of her small and elegant stature, although I'm sure she's never carried a sickle in her life. When she makes it to the Field of Reeds, she can recite a chapter from the Book of the Dead, and the shabti will come to life and do work for her, so she can enjoy other pleasures in the afterlife.

When the priest stops talking, he looks over to me to signal that it is time. I get up and stand at the head of Mom's coffin to place down the shabti and golden eagle feather. But when my finger touches Mom's coffin, a vision flashes into my mind – thick darkness, sandy deserts, and a great river nearby. My heart hammers and I pull my hand away, terrified. Goosebumps flash over my forearms, and an arctic chill creeps over the back of my neck, making my scalp crawl. *What the hell was that? It was just like my nightmare.* I take a deep breath to calm myself, trying to hide my shock.

I swallow past the lump in my throat and speak softly, picturing Mom's face. "Goodbye *neferu*" – my beautiful mother. I wrench my eyes shut and tears race down my face. I stand in silence and listen to the wind blowing through the trees. I'm surrounded by people, but it feels like I'm the last person on Earth.

When the high-pitched tones of the bagpipes play, they shake me to my core. I can't breathe in the face of such tremendous loss. When I open my eyes, Mom's coffin is being lowered into the ground.

She'll find her way to the Field of Reeds; I know she will.

I have no idea how I'll go on without her. I wish I was going with her.

Chapter 3

I stand alone in the thick darkness, waiting as a beacon for a person's ba – their soul.

I imagine this is as close to non-existence one can get. There is nothing to see, for there is nothing, only that which matters. Some people call this place Rosetjau, others, the Gateway to the Underworld.

A figure slowly emerges, displacing the darkness. She has golden skin, long black hair, is wearing sandals and a dress made of flax. Around her neck hangs a heart scarab amulet made from green jasper, and in her hands, a bouquet of lilies and lotuses.

I see myself in the reflection of her teary eyes. The head of a jackal on a man's body, golden fur, red eyes and wearing a nemes headdress and kilt. With my was scepter in one hand, I get down on one knee to lower my eyes to hers. I hold out my hand for her to take.

"O Lord Anubis, God of Embalming," she says. "I am one among you. Have I reached the Duat?"

"The Osiris Shani, your journey has just begun," I reply softly. I peer deep into the heart of Shani's ba. I see no evil, no malice, no wrongdoing, just a pure soul whose journey shall be long. "The Osiris Shani, I will lead you to your judgement, to the weighing of the heart ceremony. Prepared are you to be judged for your time in the mundane world?"

"I am prepared, Anubis."

I stand and lead the way, for I am only one of two who know the path through the thick darkness. I lead Shani to my portal, an inverted pyramidal frame made of onyx and adorned with jackal heads and fish-scale patterns of gold. Hanging in thin air, it emits a light blue hue like the skies above the twin deserts of Egypt.

I place my hand on the surface of the portal and look down at Shani. She reads my face and reaches out hesitantly, mirroring my movement. When her hand touches the surface, we're transported into the Duat. The surface of the portal is now black like ink.

We're surrounded by desert, with the great river to the south. The thick darkness has flooded the land, but it's a flood that will recede upon the arrival of Atum, the aged Sun God Ra. For even in death, Atum breathes light and warmth into the darkest of corners.

A figure approaches from the east. It is Anput – my soulmate. Like me, she has the head of a jackal and is wearing a nemes headdress, a fish-scale pattern vest and kilt. She also wears a wide necklace and mantle made of beaded carnelian, turquoise, and lapis. The red carnelian accentuates her beautiful red eyes.

I take her hand and feel whole once more. "Anput, I am honored, for I will accompany the Osiris Shani to her judgement."

Anput gets down on one knee and – through Shani's eyes – she peers into Shani's ba. "The Osiris Shani, I will accompany you also, for Anubis and I are both gods of embalming and the afterlife." Anput joins me by my side and retakes my hand.

"O Lord Anubis," Shani falters as though a deep desire is welling within.

I look down upon Shani's face. Her heart is light, but her mind heavy. "The Osiris Shani, speak your mind for you are in the presence of your shepherds, the ones that shall protect you on your journey."

"I wish to travel with Atum and his entourage upon the waters of Nun, through the Duat, to bear witness to the majesty of his rebirth."

The desire on her face makes my heart swell with joy. "If you are willing to die a second death in protection of Atum and his bark, then yes, of course," I say.

A glorious smile emerges on Shani's ba.

We head to the sandy shore where the desert meets the river, and Shani approaches the water's edge.

"The Osiris Shani, you must be careful, for the waters of Nun are dangerous."

She stops and looks back. "O Lord Anubis, why is that? I thought the waters of Nun helped rejuvenate Atum."

"You will find many things true, even if they are in opposition. Fall into the waters of Nun and you will cease to exist; you will die a second death."

Shani gasps and steps back, and then she proceeds to join Anput and I at our side.

From the east, two figures head in our direction.

Shani points. "O Lord Anubis, who are they?"

"The Osiris Shani, that is Thoth and Horus."

Horus, God of the Sky, is my half-brother. He has the head of a falcon and the body of a man. He wears the pschent crown – the Double Crown, which symbolizes Upper and Lower Egypt – a nemes headdress and a kilt with a bull's tail. Horus is the chieftain of Atum's night-bark, which is a boat called the Mesektet, and in his role of steersman, he will control the steering oar on our journey, using his razor-sharp falcon eyes to ensure a smooth passage.

Thoth, God of Reading and Writing, has the head of an ibis and the body of a man. He too wears a nemes headdress, a white sash across his chest, and a kilt. He carries a book in one hand and a reed brush in the other. I have worked alongside Thoth for many years; he assumes the role of lector priest at the weighing of the heart ceremony. His book, the Book of Thoth, which he carries with him, is full of rituals, spells, and hymns. Thoth, like Horus, is a defender of Osiris and Atum.

I bow toward them. "O Thoth, the twice great, I am honored to be in your presence once more. This is the Osiris Shani. She is a scholar like you. We will journey with you on the Mesektet to the Osiris Shani's judgment."

Thoth returns my bow and opens his long, curved black beak. "O Anubis, Anput, the honor is mine," he says, before looking down at Shani. "The Osiris Shani, you are in the great company of Anubis and Anput, gods of embalming and friends to the dead. You are most welcome in Atum's entourage."

Shani smiles with joy as she looks Thoth's ibis head over.

Horus gets down on one knee and looks Shani in the eye with his beady falcon eyes. "The Osiris Shani, we are all prepared to die a second death in the protection of Atum, the Great God – are you?"

"O Horus, God of the Sky, I am. I would gladly lay down my afterlife for Atum."

Horus bows his falcon head for a moment to acknowledge Shani's pledge.

The sky suddenly brightens, which signifies that Atum has passed through the Gap of Manu. Anput and I face the west, and as expected, the Mesektet appears on the waters of Nun. The bark is made of timber with a high prow and stern with a steering oar at the rear.

Shani, Anput, and I join Thoth and Horus by the water's edge – the thick darkness losing out to soft light.

As the Mesektet pulls up to the shore, we catch the first glimpse of the lifeless body of Atum.

Somber is this moment. The creator of all has come to the Duat to be reborn. His journey will be hard. His own demons he must face, as do we all.

The gangplank hits the desert shore, and Wepwawet, Opener of the Ways, disembarks. Like myself, he has a head of a jackal on a man's body. Not a word do we exchange, for Wepwawet is the son of Seth, and therefore is not to be trusted.

Shani looks upon his face and instinctively knows in her heart to steer clear.

I follow Shani up the gangplank, and we board the Mesektet.

The body of Atum is lifeless, bandaged from neck to toe, with only his face left visible for us to revere. In this form, he has the head of a ram on a man's body and wears a sun-disk on his head – the sun-disk is circumscribed by a golden uraeus. He lies on a reed mat atop a timber plinth. Running around the edge of the plinth is a string of shen-signs carved in intricate detail – circles with a horizontal bar beneath them, which symbolize protection and infinity.

As the gangplank is pulled aboard, Wepwawet stands on the shore and won't be joining us now that his duty has been fulfilled. Horus takes control of the steering oar and we're off.

Anput and I stand together at the gunwale and look out over the water as we journey eastward.

Shani joins Anput and me, and she stares off into the distance.

A lion, twice as tall as any god, patrols the desert. When he spots us, he heads in our direction. His long tail swishes and his mane blows in the breeze as he trots. He reaches the shore and follows at a distance, striding with purpose over the sand – his rounded ears twitching and big eyes stare.

"The Osiris Shani, it is Aker, one of the double lions. This one is called Yesterday," I say, breaking my stare with the great lion of the west.

Anput, Shani, and I watch as the lion follows. Majestic is he, fierce and strong, yet it does not do well to look at him longingly. After some time, the great lion slows to a walk and then stops, his giant frame gradually fading in the distance.

As the soft light of Atum fills the sky, the ba of many people come to the shoreline to watch us journey past. For this hour of the night their souls are rejuvenated by the presence of Atum, for even in death, the Great God creates life.

Chapter 4

I jolt awake, sending my bedsheets flying, gasping as though I just ran a marathon. I struggle to catch my breath. *What the hell was that? It was so vivid, so real.* My book on The Ennead lays splayed open on the floor, halfway across my room. That's the last time I read that before bed. As my heart rate slowly returns to normal, I think back to my dream.

I've completely lost it.

After a long weekend of doing nothing but sitting around the house, I had thought my nightmares, and the vision I had when I touched Mom's coffin, were behind me – just stress. They seem interconnected though, in some way. And if it wasn't for the vision I had at Mom's funeral, I would have just written them off as nightmares, but the vision in broad daylight has left me questioning everything. *Maybe I'm dead and this is the nightmare.* Maybe the visions are trying to tell me something about the afterlife. I shake off my mad thoughts.

After getting dressed, I walk down the hall to find Dad sitting at the kitchen bench reading the paper. I stand in front of the fireplace to warm my hands. My gaze gravitates to the dining chair Mom used to sit in; the chair that no one will ever sit in again. I stare at it a while with pain in my chest, deep in thought, until the sound of Dad turning the newspaper catches my attention.

"Why are you still here?" I ask.

"I thought I'd drop you off ... your first day back and all."

I shrug. "Whatever."

There's an awkward silence.

"Don't forget your psychiatrist's appointment this afternoon," he says as he folds up his paper.

I give him a dirty look. "I don't know why I've gotta go spill my guts to some stranger."

"Doctor Mathews recommended that you speak to someone ... and after everything you've been through, this week *and* over the past couple of years, I tend to agree."

I shake my head. If I had a normal dad, it would be him I'd talk to and not some stranger. I should have stayed in bed.

The street is lined with expensive cars, most of them European – some parents' cars, some teachers', some even belonging to seniors whose parents are already setting them up for a lifetime of greed. *Brats.* I hate this private school.

But it's Dad's old pickup truck that turns more heads than anything else – not out of envy, but disgust, from how old and beat-up it is. Although he owns the brickworks, he refuses to buy a new car. I think it's funny. I hope he never sells it, if just to piss everyone off. I grab my lunch and backpack, slamming the door shut behind me. As I walk toward the front gates, I can hear Dad's truck rumbling at idle. I picture him watching me walk in, for whatever reason, and then the gruff roar of the old vee-eight behind me tells me he's on his way.

Craig's up ahead. Like me, he's from a working-class family and doesn't have his head up his ass. He's the only seventeen-year-old I know that has braces, and they're those steely ones that look like a bear trap. The poor bastard. He always wears the latest clothes, although I suspect he does it so he doesn't get picked on so much. Me, I don't give a shit, I just wear whatever.

"Hey," he says as I approach.

As we walk up the freshly shoveled herringbone paved path, I can see him glancing over at me. I'm guessing he wants to ask about the accident, but I continue my hypnotic stare at the pavers, hoping he'll leave me alone. Our relationship is tenuous at best, and I'm always careful not to share too much with him. Afterall, there's no point in getting close to anyone, everyone I get close to dies. I notice several people staring – more people than normal, that is. Craig and I live out in the sticks and commute into Denver each day – we're like flies in a glass of overpriced champagne.

After roll call, Craig and I go to our separate classes. It's lonely going to this school. There are so few students here that I can relate to. As I near my science class, I spot Belinda coming in the opposite direction. We've only spoken a few times, but I've often romanticized about us being a couple. We're going to reach the door at the same time. Her soft skin, delicate features, and long, flowing brown hair are so arresting, for a moment in time, the whole world fades from my reality. She's wearing black shoes that border on being boots, khaki cargo pants, a vintage brown leather jacket, and as always, earrings with wrought iron nails hanging from them. She has a strange style: a conservative mix of grunge and goth. She sees me coming, and as we reach the door, I look into her brown eyes as she stares into mine. *Damn, she's beautiful.* She gives me a small smile. I nervously return it.

Mr. Tansley enters and begins our lesson. Sitting on a stool by myself at one of the lab benches, I open my books but am completely distracted. My mind races from Mom, to my nightmares and the vision, to the psychiatrist appointment this afternoon, then to thinking about Belinda, who is sitting at a nearby bench. Science is normally one of my favorite subjects, but right now, I don't want to be here.

Logan, the school bully, suddenly appears by my side, pulling me away from my thoughts and making me jump.

"Can I borrow your ruler?" he says, grabbing it off my bench. He's basically telling me he's going to take it regardless of what I have to say.

Who am I to object?

He smirks as he walks to the back of the class where he sits with his cronies.

Belinda and I make eye contact, and I quickly look away, feeling really small.

I can't get her out of my head as Mr. Tansley talks. She has this perfect mix of introversion and confidence that's near impossible to find. It's really appealing. But who am I kidding, she'd never be interested in me.

Toward the end of class, I jump up and walk to the back of the class to where Logan is. Mr. Tansley's in the back room packing away beakers and other equipment.

"Can I have my ruler back?" I ask Logan.

Logan has a stupid smirk, and – from out of nowhere – he punches me in the face. There's a solid cracking sound as my head snaps to the side. It kind of hurts, but I won't give him any satisfaction. After the week I've had, my usual fear seems to have vanished completely. I take a page out of Dad's book; I just stand there and stare, with a cast-iron poker face.

Joseph, who is sitting at the bench next to Logan and is an even bigger loser than he is, laughs really loud; it resembles appreciation. "Took it like a man!"

I feel the whole classroom staring. It's clear that Logan isn't sure what to do. He looks surprised, like he was expecting me to start balling or something.

I stare at him a second longer before turning away. I can sense Belinda looking at me, but I just gaze at the floor as I walk past her desk. A mix of emotions – loneliness, to grief, to worthlessness – come over me, and all I feel like doing is packing up my stuff and going home.

When Mr. Tansley walks back out, he doesn't even pick up on the fact that anything's happened – the class just sits in stunned silence. The bell rings and the room fills with the sound of everyone scrambling for the door.

I walk out quickly, and just as I make it to the staircase, I hear someone running up behind me. My heart speeds up when I see Belinda trying to catch up with me.

"Hey," she says, smiling as she falls into step with me. She's holding her books tight to her chest.

My pulse races as though I'm about to parachute out of a plane. "Hey," I say nervously back.

"I thought what you just did was really cool. I respect that. Logan is a dick. He's not worth getting in a fight with."

I give her a smile, trying hard to act nonchalant, but before I can think of something to say, she is speaking again.

"Sorry to hear about your mom," she says with a slight frown.

"Thanks," I reply softly.

I feel really deflated after everything that's happened and don't really know what to say. I don't know that much about her, even though she lives just down the road from us. She knocks me off balance at the best of times. We're still walking side by side when we reach the ground floor, and my heart is still running wild.

"I'll see you later, Kyle," she says with a simper and a wave.

I return her smile and wave apprehensively. "See you."

Once she's gone, I feel like a complete idiot for not talking to her more. After all, it's the first time she's ever spoken to me outside of class. I wonder if she's interested in being friends or if it's just pity, but then again, I'm sure she's being genuine. She's too down-to-earth to fake being nice. I smile inwardly. She just made my day.

After school, instead of catching the bus, I walk down the main street and turn down a side street lined with small businesses – mostly doctors' surgeries, optometrists, and dental practices. I look at the business card Dad gave me and then at the window of the building in front of me. The sign reads: Dr. Shaw – Psychiatrist.

A chime sounds when I push the door open, and soon an old guy walks out from an office at the back. He's at least sixty, has a gray beard, thinning hair, and a heavily wrinkled face. He's wearing corduroy pants and a cardigan.

"Kyle?"

I get up. "Yes, sir."

We shake hands.

"Pleased to meet you. I'm William. Did you find your way here all right?" He gestures to the hallway with an open palm, and I follow.

He holds the door open for me.

The room has the cliché couches I was expecting and a coffee table with a box of tissues in the middle. *Great, this should be a hoot.*

William gestures to one of the couches for me to sit on and he settles down on the other.

"I've spoken with Doctor Mathews, but why don't we start by you telling me a bit about yourself?"

What a crock, talking to a complete stranger about your feelings. I'd rather be home reading. I shrug. "I don't know ... I live with Dad; I'm an only child, and my mom died last week in a car accident." I realize now I will always be remembered as *that kid* who survived when his mother died in the "Conifer Crescent accident."

"I'm sorry, I can't imagine how you must be feeling. Just so I have my facts straight, that's your stepmom?"

I look William in the eye. "Yeah, that's right. But I don't think of her that way."

"Oh … sorry," William replies softly. "Why is that?"

I shrug again. "I don't know, I guess because I never knew my birth mom, I always thought of my stepmom … as just my mom."

William nods. "How have you been coping?"

"I don't know … okay. I guess."

"Have you been having any nightmares?"

My heart skips a beat. I recall the nightmare I had in the hospital of being in the Duat and seeing the portal, and the vision I had at the funeral when I touched Mom's coffin, as well as the nightmare from last night, where I was Anubis in the Duat. I don't imagine ever being able to tell him about them, although it would be good to know what they mean, whether I'm crazy or it's just stress.

"No," I state bluntly.

I'm sure William is trying hard not to show any reaction, but I notice his eyebrow twitch. I probably should have replied quicker so as to not seed any suspicion.

"Have you felt depressed at all?" he asks, scratching his beard.

I didn't really know what to expect coming to a psychiatrist for the first time, and I thought I'd put up a wall and reveal nothing, but his soft tone and look of genuine concern makes me reconsider. I guess anything I tell him would be in strict confidence. I think back to Mom's funeral and how I was wishing that I was with her, and so I decide to be honest. "Yeah."

"Any thoughts of self-harm?"

The pointed question catches me off guard. I glance up and shake my head.

"Okay, that's good. When did you start feeling depressed?"

"I don't know ... when we were in Egypt."

"And you lived there for ..." He rifles through his papers. "How long did you live in Egypt?"

"Four years. We moved there when I was eleven and then moved back just in time for year ten."

William frowns. "What was it like living there? It must have been a big cultural shock."

I nod, thinking back to all the good times we had there.

"Is that how your dad met your mom? She was Egyptian, wasn't she?"

How does he know that? I guess Doctor Mathews told him everything. I nod again.

"Tell me more about Egypt. Why did you and your dad move there?"

There's a lot of friction between Dad and me, partly due to him never being around, but I don't mind telling people his story.

"Dad owns the brickworks on the outskirts of Boulder. He was a bricklayer, started from nothing. We moved to Egypt so he could expand his business. It was only supposed to be for a year during the construction of the new plant, but then he met Mom, and before we knew it, four years had gone by. I loved it. I worked at the brickworks three days a week after school and made friends with one of the local kids, Ramsi."

"Did Ramsi speak English? I'm sure it can't have been easy to make friends there."

"I learned Arabic at the ex-pat school. That's how Dad met my mom. She was a language teacher contracting to the school from Cairo University."

"That's a good skill to have." William pauses a while as though considering his next question. "What was your relationship like with your mom?"

My heart's in pain as I picture her face, recalling her mannerisms, like how she'd stand on tiptoes to kiss me on the cheek. She was the only good thing in my life, and now she's gone. We had such a special relationship.

"We were really close. After dinner, she would sit in bed with me and tell me stories about ancient Egyptian mythology. On weekends, we'd explore; there is so much to discover in Egypt. I loved how passionate she was about her country. It was contagious."

"That's nice," William says with sincerity. "It's good to hold onto those memories. And your father ... What's your relationship like?"

"We don't have one."

William looks at me, his eyebrows ever so slightly raised. "Oh."

There's an awkward silence. The question has brought feelings of anger to the surface that I'm trying hard to suppress. "I mean, he's never home, we never talk. I have better relationships with my friends' dads than my own."

I've always dreamed of having a normal relationship with Dad. Seeing how other dads are with their kids has always been hard for me to watch.

"And you're an only child?"

I nod.

"You must have been pretty lonely when you moved to Egypt?"

I nod again, starting to feel like crap for bringing all the horrible memories of my life to the surface.

"At what point during your time in Egypt did you start getting depressed?"

I think back to our time there. "I don't know ... I guess about a year before we moved back."

"Did anything change at that point in time?" he says, scratching his beard again.

I try to recall everything that happened over there. Most of my memories of Egypt are great. But not all ...

"The only thing I can think of was ... Ramsi left. I never saw him again."

William has a look of great concentration on his face, as though he's dissecting my last words, so I try to move the conversation forward.

"It depressed the hell out of me when we moved back to the States."

William frowns heavily and then cocks his head to one side.

I explain, "I felt alienated in my own country. I was really looking forward to coming home, but once we got back, everything was different, I really struggled. I had no friends, just a few relatives. Then, to make things worse, Dad sends me to a private school. I hate it. It's full of assholes."

William chuckles. "You know, it's not uncommon to feel that way when you've spent so long away from home. I can imagine at the age you were, that feeling of alienation when you returned would be acute. Life experiences like that can be valuable, though. It gives greater insight into how the world works and builds appreciation for the things we take for granted."

I nod emphatically. "Yeah, I agree."

"Do you think your hatred for your school could be coming from the feeling of alienation?"

I know for sure I don't fit in, although I can't imagine *ever* fitting in there. "I guess. To some degree."

"Have you made many friends since moving back?"

My relationship with Craig is more one of convenience, so we're both not complete loners at school. We have so little in common. "I have *a* friend, but there's a girl I like, Belinda. I'd like to get to know better. She's not like all the others. She seems really open and caring and doesn't have an exaggerated sense of self-worth, which I find attractive."

It scares me to think about becoming close to Belinda, because everyone I've ever gotten close to has either left or died, but the dream is never far from my mind.

"What are your school marks like?"

"Poor. Science is the only class I care about."

"Why is that?"

"It's the only subject that interests me. Plus, Belinda's in it."

The more we chat, the more at ease I feel. I was unsure at first, but William seems like a stand-up guy; he's laid back, sincere, and I feel like I can trust him. His heavily wrinkled face, I imagine, reflects a long hard life, and I wonder what stories he could tell me.

At the end of the session, he hands me a prescription.

"What's this for?"

"They're antidepressants. I'd like you to try them."

I read the prescription. "I'm not taking medication."

"Why is that?" he asks.

I open my mouth and am about to say, "because there's nothing wrong with me," but I can't bring myself to say it.

"Some people have no response to antidepressants, but for some, finding the right antidepressant can have a real psychopharmacological effect. It's worth pursuing;

sometimes they can make the difference between life and death. We might not find one that works for you on the first go, but it's definitely worth trying, considering everything you've been through." William pauses and gives me a sympathetic smile. "Will you try them?"

I glance up and nod, a slow realization sinking in that I need help. "I guess."

After William sees me out, I head toward the Denver library. I'm not feeling ready to go home just yet, and the vision at Mom's funeral and the nightmares are beginning to plague my thoughts. They were so similar they must be related, surely. My grip on reality feels like it's slipping. I wonder if the visions are actually religious delusions. Anubis was a God of Embalming, after all, and the one who would weigh a soul's heart against the feather of Maat.

I wonder whether I could find a book on the subject, and climb the steps to the library, knocking the snow off my shoes before entering. I often come here to borrow books, so head straight for the timber cabinets with the paper index cards and start flicking through them.

"Can I help you?" an older lady asks, startling me.

"Oh … no. Thank you," I reply, not wanting to tell her what I'm looking for, and certainly not *why*.

She smiles and ambles off.

I finally find some book titles on religious psychology and head in the general direction of the shelves.

I pull a book off the shelves that has a hard cover and is as thick as a brick. It's titled *Psychological Characteristics of Religious Delusions*. It doesn't look like it's ever been opened. Egyptian mythology is really a misnomer, it should be called Egyptian religion, and I hope this book can help.

It was Mom who taught me most of what I know about ancient Egyptian mythology. But she would feel guilty as hell for telling me mythological stories before bedtime, because I often had nightmares. I'd always beg her to tell me more though. I guess she loved those times as much as me.

Dad was never around at bedtime, of course.

I'm feeling completely alone again, and now – afraid of going to sleep of a night – I feel like my world is falling apart. An all-new low for me. I wish I could just be a normal kid, with normal problems, and have a dad that was there for me when I needed him.

Chapter 5

Anput and I stand at the gunwale, each with a hand on Shani's shoulders as she stands between us. I look down at the top of Shani's head as she takes in the view. The river is wide with alcoves of reeds. The pace of the waters of Nun flowing from west to east is like that of a gentle breeze. In the distance, parched fields of wheat and barley sway in the breeze. People stand at the shoreline with open palms raised toward the lifeless body of Atum. It is indeed an honor to be in his entourage.

Thoth is standing in the prow of the Mesektet reading his book. When the bark suddenly changes course, his ibis head looks up. I follow his stare to find the twin goddesses, Isis and Nephthys, standing at the shore some distance away. I look over my shoulder as Horus controls the steering oar. In his normal form, that of a man with the head of a falcon, naught can escape his razor-sharp eyes.

Isis, Goddess of Magic and Spells, wears a long red dress and a gold mantel beaded with carnelian, turquoise, and lapis. She is indeed beautiful. Nephthys, Goddess of Death and Decay and a friend to the dead, wears a long green dress. She also wears a beaded gold mantel and has a truly elegant walk.

I point to the goddesses. "The Osiris Shani, they are the twin goddesses Isis and Nephthys."

"Your stepmother and mother," Shani says, beaming.

"That is correct," I reply.

My mother Nephthys has always lived in the shadow of my stepmother, Isis. I see in her face and in the way she carries herself that she feels like she doesn't measure up to her.

We pull over to the shore, and Isis and Nephthys board the Mesektet.

"O Lord Anubis," Isis says, "have thou heard about the theft of the hearts?"

My heart sinks at the mention of such an occurrence. "I have not."

"Two souls, Aya and Eman, have had their hearts stolen; they have not long entered the Duat."

"Who would do such a thing?" Anput asks in disgust.

72

"I do not understand," I add, reading Nephthys' face, then Isis', for more insight. "Anput and I prepared Aya and Eman together."

"Tau," Nephthys says. "Tau ... the thief entered the Duat not so long ago. Maybe he stole the hearts."

Deeply troubling this news is. I look my mother in the eye.

Isis also looks Nephthys in the eye. "Yes ... maybe. On our journey, we will seek out Tau and question him, we shall."

Shani's concern rises to the surface of her features.

I get down on one knee. "The Osiris Shani, what is troubling you?"

"O Lord Anubis, what will be Tau's fate?"

"If a thief indeed he is, then he will fail his weighing of the heart ceremony. At best, he will be doomed to wander restless for eternity; at worst, he will be annihilated in the Island of Fire."

Shani looks at me with fear in her eyes.

"A fitting end to a life spent ill on Earth, is it not?" I ask.

Shani looks at the deck before our eyes meet again. "I guess."

Isis and Nephthys stand beside the lifeless body of Atum as we continue our journey eastward. The twin goddesses will protect him and his bark at all costs. Their presence always brings me great comfort.

I place my hand on my soulmate's waist. "O Anput, have you thought about why Aya's and Eman's hearts would be stolen?"

She places her hand on my forearm. "I have ... however, I cannot comprehend such an act or its purpose."

I close my eyes and search my heart. Never before has such an atrocity been committed. My heart and mind are clouded to the truth. Looking into her red eyes, I exhale heavily. "My soulmate, the truth we will discover. But I fear most of all, we will be too late in discovering for whatever purpose their hearts are required."

Isis leaves Atum's side and joins us. She is my father Osiris' sister-wife, and although not my birthmother, she raised me as her own.

"O Lord Anubis," she says, "I have used magic to call for the Great Bennu Bird to seek his wisdom. For we must discover the thief of Aya's and Eman's hearts."

I bow. "O Isis, my goddess, we will discover the truth before this night is out, for that you have my word."

Shani looks up and catches my eye again. Something weighs on her mind, but I cannot enquire further, for the sound of thudding of air can be heard. We look to the sky. The Great Bennu Bird flaps his wings as he descends, his twig-like legs reaching out. Gracefully landing on the gunwale, he folds his wings in neatly and his long thin neck folds into an S.

"O Great Bennu Bird," Isis says, bowing her head in reverence, "we seek your wisdom."

"O Isis, Mistress of Magic, Speaker of Spell, you spoke, and I came forth," he says, his expression containing great sorrow. "Though I am the bringer of terrible news. Two souls, that have not long entered the Duat, have had their hearts stolen."

"O Great Bennu Bird, we have heard about Aya and Eman. Greatly troubled are we by this news. Their hearts must be found and returned unto them before this night is out. I called upon thou, for it is your wisdom we seek."

The Great Bennu Bird glances between us. "You are wise to seek my council; however, you must seek a higher council. Go to Heh, God of Eternity, for he has seen all that was, is, and has yet to pass."

Isis, Anput, and I bow in reverence to the Great Bennu Bird, before he spreads his wings and thuds the air, rising higher and higher. We're watching him fly away when I hear soft footsteps behind us, soft footsteps of a goddess.

We turn around to find that Nephthys has joined us.

"Nephthys, what makes thou think it is Tau that stole the hearts of Aya and Eman?" Isis asks.

Now standing alongside each other, the twin goddesses look identical in every way, except for the color of their dresses.

"The languid one, Tau, is a thief and a liar," Nephthys says. "He entered the Duat of this night, the same night as Aya and Eman. What other truth could there be?"

"That is what we must find out," Isis says, deep in thought.

"We are ahead for this hour of the night; may I suggest we pull in and rest upon shore," I say.

Isis bows to me in acknowledgment, and Horus steers toward shore. When the gangplank is deployed, there are a great many people on the shore standing in adoration of Atum. Isis, Shani, and I walk down the gangplank in single file and stand on the sandy shore.

Shani frowns. The heaviness is clearly still within her mind. "O Lord Anubis, what will happen to Aya and Eman if their hearts are not returned?"

I get down on one knee, so our eyes are at the same height, and steady myself with my was scepter – the scepter of power. "If they reach the eastern akhet, the eastern junction where the subterranean and celestial spheres meet, they may enter the Hall of the Two Truths and declare their innocence. They will have their heart scarabs weighed against the feather of Maat, and if they are found to have lived a pure life in the mundane world, they may enter the Field of Reeds, as will you."

"Will they be able to go-forth-by-day? Will they be reunited with their kas?"

I shake my head. "The Osiris Shani, a person's ba, their soul, must retain its heart in the Duat, just as the physical body must in the mundane world. They will be able to enter the Field of Reeds, but there, they must remain, until their hearts are returned. While their kas, their life forces, may reside close to their tombs on Earth, it is their ba's hearts that must be returned before they can go-forth-by-day, to enjoy another day on Earth with their loved ones."

Sadness falls on Shani's face as the words leave my lips. She looks into my eyes. "Anubis, what of Tau, what will happen to him if he fails his weighing of the heart ceremony?"

"At best, Tau will wander the Duat restless for eternity; at worst, he will be forced to serve in Sokar's army or be tossed into the Island of Fire."

Shani's jaw drops open. "O Lord Anubis, I wish so much to pass my judgement and to enter into the Field of Reeds, to dwell with the blessed dead, but ..."

"Fear not, the Osiris Shani, for I am your shepherd," I say. "Pray tell, what is on your mind?"

Shani looks down, her face growing with sadness again. "When I was just a little girl ... I was playing with my friends, our neighbor's kids. At their home. I was hungry ... and ..." Words seem to elude Shani. I place my hand on her shoulder to comfort her, and she continues. "I ... I ate an apple, without asking. I stole!"

"The Osiris Shani, if your friends took food from your parents without asking, would you consider that theft?"

Shani searches her feelings with a heavy brow. "I ... I guess not. It would be rude, but not stealing."

"Then you have naught to worry about."

"But ... what if *they* considered it theft? What if I don't believe in my heart that I am innocent? How can I declare my innocence to the forty-two deities in the Hall of the Two Truths, if in my heart, I don't believe it?"

"Only you can decide what to declare to the forty-two deities, but I warn you, whatever you say, they will know the truth. In that moment, above all else, you must speak the truth, as it is in your heart."

Shani nods.

"O Lord Anubis," Isis says as she approaches. "We must continue our journey."

I stand and hold my hand out for Shani to take. We walk up the gangplank and join the others. As the Mesektet pulls away from the shore, the twin goddesses, Isis and Nephthys, take up their spots alongside Atum, and we are on our way.

"O Lord Anubis," Shani says as she looks up at the prow. "I would ever so like to converse with Thoth, God of Reading and Writing."

"Then we shall." I take her hand and lead her to the prow.

Thoth turns to face us. With the head of an ibis on a man's body, he is as tall as me. He looks down upon Shani's face, which has now lit up with a beautiful smile. "The Osiris Shani, would you like to behold the Book of Thoth?"

Shani's smile swells with joy. "O Lord Thoth, I would be honored." She takes Thoth's hand and together they

stand before the lectern, upon which sits the great book –
the Book of Thoth.

Thoth begins to recite from the pages, and while
Shani takes in every word that leaves his long black beak,
I turn to face Anput. We share a joyful smile. Shepherding
the ba of the blessed dead through the Duat brings us so
much joy, I feel honored for every night we have the
privilege.

When Shani steps down from the prow and joins us,
she is beaming.

"O Lord Anubis, thank you. Conversing with Thoth
has made my heart warm with delight."

We stand alongside the timber plinth where Atum
lays, and we revere in his majesty. He is a sight to behold.
When the Great Scarab joins himself to Atum, and when
we reach the eastern akhet, Atum will be reborn as
Khepri, the morning sun. Then, when the new day is born,
he will rise high into the sky and become Ra, his greatest
of forms, and breathe life into the mundane world.

"O Lord Anubis, I wish to help find those guilty of
stealing Aya's and Eman's hearts," Shani says, before
casting an inquiring frown toward Isis, who stands beside
the lifeless body of Atum. "If I were to ask, would Isis
bestow upon me magic?"

I bow toward her and take her hand, leading her over to Isis.

Shani hesitates before the great goddess, and then makes her request.

"The Osiris Shani," Isis says, "in the entourage of Atum, your presence isn't merely *enough*, your assistance is *required*." Isis places her palms on Shani's cheeks and pulls her head forward in a bow. Isis too bows until her forehead touches Shani's. "The Osiris Shani, for use in the Underworld while in Atum's entourage, I bestow upon thou akhu."

A blinding blue light emanates from the point where their foreheads touch. I hold my palm up to shield my eyes. Through clenched eyelids, the light feels like it's passing right through me unobstructed.

Chapter 6

The blinding lights of an oncoming car make me jerk in fright. With my heart hammering, I watch through the bus windows as it speeds by. *What the hell just happened?* Another nightmare, but had I fallen asleep? I remember getting on the bus in Denver, but now I'm nearly home. *Did I blackout?* Was that a daytime vision, a delusion? It's been several weeks since my last nightmare, and I was hoping they had gone away, but it seems like they're becoming more intrusive. Blurring the lines between the mundane world and the afterlife.

As much as I wish I was heading to visit Mom's grave, instead of going home, I have been putting it off because of the vision I had when I touched her coffin. I shake my head, trying to clear my mad thoughts.

I step off the bus and my feet crunch in the snow. I cross the road, trying hard to not look at the skid marks. I'm slowly getting used to being at home; however, walking over the patch of road where Mom was stolen from me is still excruciating.

Mid-winter and the sun has already set. It's not even dinner time. I've just unlocked the front door when I hear the rumble of a vee-eight on the road. It doesn't quite sound the same as Dad's truck, plus it's too early to be him. I throw my backpack inside the house and then walk back to the corner of the house to see who it is. Uncle Tim is driving down the driveway in his old Mustang – it's sounding sicker than usual with a screeching coming from the engine.

I smile. "Uncle Tim."

"Hey, Kyle. How's it going?"

"Good, your Mustang doesn't sound too good though."

"Na. It's spun a camshaft bearing this week."

I look it over. "Are you still thinking about selling it?"

Uncle Tim raises his eyebrows. "Yeah. I've already bought a new Mustang ... be ready for pickup in a few days."

"How much are you asking for your old one?"

"I don't know ..." he says, thinking on it for a second. "About five hundred bucks. It would cost another fifteen hundred to two thousand to rebuild the engine, though. Personally, I don't see it's worth it."

"Oh." I'm a little disappointed. It may be old, but it's still a nice ride. I can picture taking Belinda for a ride in it.

I think Uncle Tim notices the dismay in my face and says, "But you know ... I have a workshop manual for it. It has a step-by-step guide of how to rebuild the engine. I'm sure a smart kid like you could work it out, plus I could drop by from time to time and give you a hand."

"Are you serious?" I ask, starting to get excited about fixing it up. "That sounds hard. How much would the parts cost?" I can't help but wonder whether rebuilding the engine with Dad's help would bring Dad and me closer.

"Probably about a thousand. How much do you have?"

"I've got just over two thousand saved up."

"How did you get that kind of money together?" He laughs. "I know you didn't get it from my brother!"

I smile. "Most of it I saved from working at the brickworks in Cairo."

"Ah, right."

"So, can I buy it off you then?"

Uncle Tim smiles at the excitement in my eyes. "I don't see why not." He spins around when Dad turns into the driveway, a good hour or two before schedule.

When I see Dad's face as he pulls up, the fantasy of us working on the engine together slowly evaporates. I know he'll shoot me down, just like he always does.

Dad climbs out of his old pick-up and slams the door. He mostly works in the office now, but he still wears steel-capped boots and jeans. As he and Uncle Tim catch up, I walk around the Mustang, taking a closer look, wondering how much work it would need.

When their conversation has come to an end, Uncle Tim looks at me. I guess prompting me to bring up the car to my dad.

"Uncle Tim is selling his Mustang. I was going to buy it and rebuild the engine."

Dad frowns. "What do *you* know about engines?"

He's such an ass.

"I've got a workshop manual for it, and I can drop by and give him a hand from time to time," Uncle Tim says.

You have to be really skilled in reading Dad's minimal facial expressions to detect it, but I can see his disapproval coming to the surface of his features. "Whatever," he says, shaking his head.

"So … I can buy it then?"

"It's your money!" Dad replies gruffly.

I run into the house, smiling, and pull out my lockbox from under my bed where I keep my savings. I count out five hundred dollars.

Outside, I can hardly wipe the smile off my face as I hand Uncle Tim the money. I can't believe this. *This is going to be awesome.* My first car. He pulls his keys out of his pocket and takes one off and hands it to me. The old key is all metal with the Ford logo raised on the surface. My mind goes into overdrive, imagining going for my first drive by myself, asking Belinda out on a date.

"Don't you need it until your new car arrives?" I ask.

Uncle Tim shakes his head. "Na. Your dad can give me a lift home. It's all yours."

"I hope you know what you've gotten yourself into," Dad says, looking displeased.

Uncle Tim, on the other hand, pats me on the shoulder and we both grin.

After dinner, I head out through the garage to look at *my* car. It's a '72 Mustang Fastback. The red paint is faded, as are the black stripes, and it has rust holes in the doors and sills, but I don't care. It still looks awesome. I crack open the driver's side door and climb in. It has a strong smell of old leather and what must be at least twenty years of dirt and grime. The steering wheel's all cracked, as is the dash.

I'd love to take it for a drive right now, but I better not, Dad would shit bricks if I went out at night.

I turn the key. The old vee-eight roars to life with a heavy screech that quietens after a few seconds. I drive it into the garage and kill the engine. My smile fades as I think about parking in Mom's spot. I feel for the feather of Maat amulet under my shirt. I picture her smiling face, and my heart aches.

Dad walks out. "I'm just taking Tim home. Back in an hour or so."

I nod as I climb out, and then an idea forms in my mind. "Can I drive to school tomorrow?"

"No!" Dad says, pursing his lips as he throws on his jacket.

"But I wanted to drive to school just once before pulling the engine—"

Dad fixes me with a stare. "What did I *just* say?"

I shut up. When he's like this, the conversation never ends well. Uncle Tim walks back out. It doesn't seem as if he overheard us, but maybe he's just good at hiding it. "Thanks, Uncle Tim. I love the car."

"Just take it easy, buddy. Even with the engine in the condition it's in, it still has a fair amount of power."

"I will. Thanks."

I watch as Dad's pick-up trundles up the driveway, lighting up the snow and slush. He pulls out onto the road and slowly drives off. Once they're out of sight, I turn and look at my car, and I'm overcome with guilt for feeling joy when Mom has not long died. I wish my emotions would stop swinging wildly from one extreme to another.

Sitting in the Mustang the following morning on my way to school, my heart's beating hard. I've driven it to the top of our driveway, the old vee-eight engine rumbling under the hood. For once, I didn't care that Dad had left for work before I even got up, and even though he's going to kill me for driving it when he said no, screw it, it'll be months before the Mustang's up and running again once I start pulling it to pieces. And if I get back from school before he gets back from work as usual, he won't even find out.

I look both ways half a dozen times before slowly pulling out, extremely aware of the stretch of road with the skid marks. I barely touch the gas with my foot, but the back of the car slides sideways a few inches and I can hear the tires slowly spinning in the slush. *Damn*. Uncle Tim was right, this thing's a brute. Once the car straightens up, I ever so slowly accelerate.

A light snow begins to fall as I'm driving into the city. It's so strange driving alone, especially after spending so many hours with Mom giving me lessons while I was on my learner's permit. I turn the wipers on, but only one of them springs to life. At least it's the driver's side. I picture what it would be like having Belinda sit beside me, instead of being all alone. I imagine what it would feel like driving down the road with us holding hands.

When I get to school, there's the normal procession of expensive European cars. *Would it kill them to buy American?* Feeling proud to be driving a car that was built here, I carefully park out front. I grab my backpack and jump out, locking the door behind me. Craig's walking down the footpath, and I race across the street to catch up.

"Is that your uncle's car?" he asks, frowning in confusion. "Why are you driving it?"

I grin. "It's mine now. I bought it."

His eyes widen. "Holy shit! Does your dad know what size engine it has?"

I don't even know what size it is other than it's a vee-eight, but I don't know about Dad. He could know all about engines and I wouldn't have a clue.

As we walk in the front gates, I suddenly feel an overwhelming sense of depression. I hate this place; it toxifies my soul. There's something deeply troubling about being surrounded by so many people and yet still feeling all alone. Craig's a nice guy and all, but even when I'm around him I still feel alone. I can't wait to get out of here and start my own life. I think back to what William was saying about feeling alienated. He's probably right. Maybe I do hate the kids here because I'm not one of them, but then, maybe they're just assholes. Probably a bit of both, I guess.

It's the last class of the day and I'm excited about driving home. The room slowly fills as I sit at one of the lab benches by myself, wishing this class will pass quickly. When Logan and Joseph walk in, Logan and I make eye contact before he quickly looks away. I can imagine he's probably a little intimidated after I didn't react to him punching me, or at least wary of me. It's almost like I took away his power.

Belinda enters the room and approaches me. My heart skips a beat.

"Do you mind if I sit here?" she asks.

My heart nearly jumps out of my throat. "No, of course not." Damn, she stirs up some deep feelings. My heart's pounding.

She drops her books on the bench and pulls out a stool to sit on. "I saw you this morning arrive in a red Mustang, it that yours?"

I nod, smiling.

"That's cool. What engine does it have?"

Her question catches me completely off guard. Why would she care? But at least I've already been faced with this question once today, so I don't have to scramble for the answer. "It's a vee-eight."

Belinda swivels on her stool to face me. "What color's the engine?"

"It's red."

"It's a three fifty-one then ... Cleveland."

What the hell. How does she know that?

Belinda reads my face. "Dad's a mechanic."

"Oh." I suddenly recall seeing an old Camaro and an Impala rusting away out the back of her place, so that makes sense. I smile.

We sit quietly waiting for Mr. Tansley to turn up. I try to think of something to say. "The engine spun a bearing. I drove it in today, as it's my last chance for a while. I'm going to start pulling the engine out on the weekend. I'm going to rebuild it myself."

Belinda's eyes light up. "Aw ... nice!"

I wouldn't have imagined her knowing heaps about cars, but now I know she has a dad that's a mechanic, she probably knows more than me. I wonder if she'd think I was hitting on her if I asked for her help. After having her sit next to me and seeing how her eyes light up with excitement, I figure it can't hurt to ask.

My heart speeds up and I try hard to sound nonchalant. "Would you like to help?"

Her eyes widen. "Hell yeah. I'd love to."

I can't believe she said yes; that I'll get to spend time with her outside of school. "Do you know much about engines?" I ask as respectfully as I can, so I don't sound like my dad.

"I know my way around an engine bay. Dad has taught me a lot."

I would never normally ask, but with how receptive she's been, I venture my next question. "Can I give you a lift home after school?"

Belinda's simper just about melts my heart.

"Sure, I'd like that."

After class, Belinda and I walk toward my car, each of us caught up in silent contemplation. I'm so excited that I'm giving her a lift home and that she'll help me with the Mustang, but I still can't escape the feeling that something bad will happen, that I'll lose her too if we get close.

A couple of her friends, who are standing around on the front grass, call out to her as they wave goodbye. The smirks on their faces are clear, even from this distance. Belinda's eyes are glued to the ground, and she is blushing. When she finally looks up when we reach my car, our eyes meet, both of us trying hard to suppress our grins.

As I insert the key into the door, I see Logan approach, his fifty-thousand-dollar import parked several spots up.

"Nice rust bucket," he calls out.

Belinda gives him a dirty look as I slide into the driver's seat. I unlock the passenger's side and Belinda jumps in.

Logan makes a display of pressing his key remote, unlocking his car with several loud high-pitched beeps.

"Ignore that moron," Belinda says with a steely face. "I'd rather ride in an American muscle car any day than his plastic heap of crap."

Her dad has obviously had a big influence on her interest in cars. The thought must be showing on my face because she suddenly asks, "What?" surveying my face.

I shake my head, smiling. "Nothing."

As we leave the city, I notice Belinda has her arms knitted together.

I turn up the heat. "Sorry, are you cold?"

"That's okay," she replies softly. "It's one of the things I like about old cars ... they have character."

We share a smile.

I can't believe Belinda is here with me right now. Just this morning, I was picturing us driving along, holding hands. I've never had a girlfriend, but even I know it's too soon for that. I'm not going out on that limb until I know she'd be receptive. But still, having her here with me is pretty awesome.

Belinda looks deep in thought when I turn onto Conifer Crescent.

"Do you have many tools ... to pull your engine out?" Belinda asks.

"Dad's got a big tool chest. It's pretty old but well stocked."

"Do you have an engine stand or hoist?"

I glance over, not having really thought about it or knowing what I'll need. "No."

"Dad's got both. I'm sure he wouldn't mind lending them to you."

As we approach her house, my mind's going a million miles an hour. *What are her parents like? Will they approve of me driving her home? Will they approve of me?* I've gone past her house hundreds of times before, and ever since I've been back, I've wondered what it would feel like turning into her driveway.

"How big's your property?" I ask, trying to engage her in conversation to distract myself from my nerves.

"Five acres. Dad bought it out of his compo."

I try to read Belinda's face, not really sure what "compo" means.

"He was in an accident at work. A jack collapsed, and a car fell on him. Broke his back and he can't work anymore. He got a payout from the insurance. It took him years just to walk again."

"Oh. That's not good," I say, feeling like I can relate to her not having lived the "white picket fence" fairytale life that so many at our school try to exude.

Belinda's mouth twitches into a faint smile as she jumps out.

Now I'm here, I'm scared stiff. I hope her parents are as nice as her. Her house is small with a shingle roof, weather boards and verandas on all sides. Out the back, there's a huge steel shed filled with cars and parts.

"Hey Dad," Belinda calls out when we step in the front door.

Her house is a bit of a dump, although I can't talk. Our house isn't much better. There are even car parts in the house. Her dad is sitting in a tattered armchair in the living room. He's a little overweight and has a graying beard and thinning hair.

"Hey sweetie," he says and glances at me. "Is that your Mustang, son?"

I smile. "Yes, sir."

"*Nice!*" he replies enthusiastically.

Belinda's mouth curves upward and I relax a little, knowing I'll likely have something in common with her dad. I was preparing myself for a more hostile greeting – I guess based on the way my dad is toward people.

Her dad struggles out of his armchair, leaning on a four-pronged walking cane to help him.

"This is Kyle, Dad."

He hobbles over and shakes my hand. "How's it going?"

"Good, sir."

"Enough with the sirs. Just call me Warren."

Nothing like Dad!

After our introductions, I get twenty questions: where I live and what Dad does for a living. I can already tell where the conversation's going when Warren's face hardens.

"Sorry to hear about your mom," he says.

"Thanks," I reply somberly, the pain still raw.

The three of us exchange silent glances, and I look to Belinda in an effort to change topic.

"Can Kyle borrow an engine stand and the hoist, Dad? He's going to rebuild his Mustang's engine."

"Yeah ... sure. No problem at all. Say, why don't you stay for dinner, and afterward I can follow you home in my truck to drop the gear off?"

I glance over at Belinda and then back at her dad, surprised by the offer. Dad won't be home for hours, and I was only going to have a microwave dinner, anyway. "I'd like that. Thank you ... Warren."

He smiles with his eyes when I use his name, then looks at his watch. "Come and show me your car, son."

After he shuffles past, Belinda is beaming at me, almost blushing.

After dinner, we load her dad's truck up with the engine stand and hoist. Warren slowly climbs into his truck, and Belinda and I jump into my Mustang.

"Why's your house dark?" Belinda asks as we drive down my driveway. "Where's your dad?"

"He's not home yet."

I just make out her head jerking back an inch. In surprise, I guess.

After Belinda and I unload the stand and the hoist, Warren stops before climbing back into his truck and says, "If you need a hand, son, just ask. I can't lift anything heavy, but I'd be happy to help in any way."

"Thank you, Warren."

Belinda smiles ingratiatingly and waves as she climbs into her dad's truck. I return the wave, feeling completely beside myself with how well today went.

When they make it to the top of the driveway, I see Dad's truck come down the road. He has to stop to let them out. *Great. This should be fun.* My Mustang's still out, a sure sign I've driven it, and with someone else's workshop equipment now in the garage, he's probably going to go off. But I'm not going to hide the fact I drove today, stuff him.

After he parks in the garage, he climbs out, looks the stand and hoist over and gives me a strong look. "Was that Warren Andrews' truck pulling out of the driveway? Is that his gear?"

"Yeah."

"He's a bum. I don't want you hanging around with his daughter; she's bad news."

I'm sick of him being so critical of everyone and everything.

"What would you know?" I raise my voice. "You don't know anything about them."

"You're not hanging around her, got it?" He looks at my Mustang, which is still sitting in the driveway. "Did you drive that when I told you not to?"

"Yeah. And nothing happened. I can look after myself."

Dad's pursed lips make him look like he's trying to stop himself from blowing a gasket. I can see him calculating whether to throw more fuel on the fire or leave it. A tense few seconds pass before he shakes his head and walks inside.

Once he's gone, I realize how fast my hearts going; I exhale and loosen my shoulders.

After putting my car away, I have a quick shower and head to my bedroom. Dad has a talent for turning a good day upside down. I'm sick of these wild swings between hope and despair, joy and depression. With my mood suddenly turning dark, I worry about going to sleep. I pull the book about religious delusions off my shelves and sit on the end of my bed. I have no idea what my visions mean, and while I'm afraid to find out, I have to know; I have to find the answers.

Chapter 7

After spending most of the day stripping parts off my Mustang's engine, getting it ready to pull out, Belinda and I are both covered in grease and dirt. She's such a tomboy. Her earrings that are made of wrought iron nails make sense, now I can see her elbows deep, working on a car.

Her pink lips, cute nose, and long eyelashes give her such a striking beauty, it's in stark contrast to the dirty, greasy work of swings spanners and busting knuckles. It's refreshing that she's so different to most girls, yet it's still surreal she's helping with my car.

The only thing holding the engine in the car are the engine mounts and half a dozen bolts to the transmission. With the bonnet off and the hoist chained to the engine, the back end of the car hangs out over concrete. I look at the time – it's too late in the day to start pulling the engine out now.

But I don't want our time to end just yet, so I try to think of an excuse to spend more time with her.

"Do want to go for a walk?" Belinda asks before I can say anything.

I'm taken aback; she's often quite forward. I nod, trying to hide my enthusiasm.

We head inside to get washed up. The laundry room's pretty rough with old wallpaper and hideous green tiles, but after seeing her house, I'm not so worried about what she might think.

"Where's your dad?" she asks.

"At work."

Belinda looks at me with a slight frown.

I stick my head out of the laundry room to read the clock at the end of the hall. "He'll be home soon ... ish." Then I ask, "Have you rebuilt an engine before?"

"No. I've helped at various stages, but I've never rebuilt a complete engine."

It's late in the day and no doubt freezing cold outside, so I grab my jacket. "Where did you want to go?"

Belinda smiles. "It's a bit of a hike, but do want to walk down to the lake behind my place?"

"Yeah. Sounds good."

I hear Dad's truck outside, and the garage door starts opening on his side. Dad drives in, climbs out and slams his door. He's often like a bear with a sore head, but on weekends it's usually worse. He looks at all the car parts and plastic containers filled with bolts strewn across the bench.

"This is Belinda," I say.

He looks at Belinda sideways and mutters a feeble greeting.

Almost imperceptibly, Belinda's head jerks back in reaction to Dad's bluntness. She waves nervously. "Hi, Mr. Roberts."

He doesn't respond to her and turns to head inside. I shake my head as he closes the door behind him, letting Belinda know it's not her fault.

As we head down the road toward Belinda's place, I look to the west where the sun is vaguely masked by a wisp of a cloud. In another hour or so, the sun will set behind the mountains, and I wonder if I'll have another nightmare tonight. I guess it could be worse, I could have a vision while with Belinda. That would make her run for the hills.

"What?" she asks curiously, catching me off guard; I guess I must have been staring.

I try to think of something to say. "Where did you get earrings like that?"

"My uncle's a blacksmith. He helped me make the nails, and then I soft soldered them to a pair of hoop earrings I already had. Do you like them?"

"Yeah, they're different."

When we make it to Belinda's, we walk past her house and head toward the rear of the property. I spot her dad in the shed rummaging through car parts. "Hi, Warren," I call out and wave.

"Hi, Kyle, how's it going? Got the engine out yet?"

"Not quite, I'm going to pull it out in the morning."

"Belinda will give you a hand, won't you, sweetie?" he says as he hobbles over on his walking cane.

Belinda smiles. "Yeah, sure. We're just going for a walk down to the lake."

"All right. Be safe."

Once we're out of earshot, I say to Belinda, "I was going to ask for your help to pull the engine out anyway, but why did your dad ask you to help me? I wouldn't have thought he'd want you hanging around boys much."

Belinda shakes her head. "He's not like that. He's a realist, and besides, he likes you."

I snap my head toward her. "What? He said that?"

Belinda laughs. "Yeah. He said anyone that drives an American muscle car and is willing to get their hands dirty is okay in his book."

We both laugh. I'm sure she's overexaggerating, but it's nice to know he's not going to chase me off with a shotgun.

When we make it to the rear fence, Belinda grabs hold of the barbwire and spreads it apart for me to climb through. I smile at her tomboyish ways.

"What?" Belinda asks, catching me again.

"Nothing," I say, before stepping through the fence.

I turn back and spread the wire so she can step through. When I let go, she playfully shoves me with both hands. I laugh as I stumble sideways in the snow. Belinda's glowing, although it's probably more the cold that's causing her cheeks to turn red.

I want to reach out and hold her hand, but refrain. Belinda can be quite forward, and I suspect she'd be receptive, but with how much trouble I have making friends, I don't want to risk making the wrong decision and ruining what we have.

When we make it to the lake, Belinda sits on a boulder and looks out over the icy water and the surrounding snowy woods. There's room, so I take the gamble she won't mind me sitting next to her and plonk myself down.

"I come down here in summer," she says. "It's really beautiful. I love swimming in the summer heat and then lying around drying in the sun."

I give her a smile. Thinking about the sun reminds me of my last memory of Mom, when she was praising Khepri. I reckon Mom would have liked Belinda. If Dad gave her half a chance, he probably would too. The fear of getting close to Belinda and then having something go horribly wrong and losing her, is slowly being eroded by the sheer joy of being in her company.

Belinda leans against me. It's unexpected, but I don't show it. I turn my head, as does she. My heart melts when she looks into my eyes – it's like she's looking right into my soul. I don't know what it is, but it feels like we're soulmates from another life. I get the same feeling when I'm around Anput in the Duat. All I want to do is kiss her, but I can tell there's something on her mind.

"What's wrong?" I ask.

She looks down. "Doesn't your dad like me?"

I feel gutted by the question. Seeing the way Warren is with Belinda, and even toward me, shines an even harsher spotlight on Dad and the poor relationship I have with him. If even I don't feel wanted by Dad, how could Belinda possibly feel wanted by him?

"He just doesn't know you," I say, trying to excuse his shortcomings. "Don't take it personally. He's like that to everyone." As the words leave my mouth, I try to read Belinda's reaction. She sits quietly, clearly mulling over my words. I pull my jacket in close to protect myself from the chilly air, thinking about Dad and his blunt, emotionless greeting to her. He better not drive her away. I'd never forgive him.

Belinda looks pensive, like she's considering her next question. "What was your mom like?" she asks softly.

I glance over. "The polar opposite of Dad. I don't how they ended up together. I must be missing something. She was so kind ... would help anyone. She was such a beautiful soul."

"I've seen you and your mom around town. She was Egyptian, wasn't she?"

I swallow hard, trying not to show how much the memory of her is affecting me. "Yeah."

"I can't imagine how you must be feeling," she says solemnly.

I want to open up to Belinda, to bring us closer, but I'm scared to tell her about the dark thoughts and feeling I have inside. I decide to take a chance and share something with her that I've never told anyone. "I've always wondered why I've never had any strong feelings toward my birth mom. I've never felt like I loved her. I guess Dad never talking about her doesn't help."

Belinda has sadness in her eyes. "Do you think you loved your mom more because you never knew your birth mom and because of the way your dad is?"

I think on Belinda's words a while before nodding, blinking away my tears. "I guess I did put all my eggs in one basket and loved my mom whole heartedly."

Belinda looks longingly out over the water.

Still waters run deep, I think to myself. I suspect there's far more to her than what I've seen – a deeper side, maybe even a spiritual side.

"Do you believe in the soul?" I ask.

Belinda looks intensely at me. "Yeah. I think that the things people do in life, how they treat one another, is a reflection of their soul, and that allows you to see their true self. Are you thinking about your mom?"

"Yeah ... I picture her soul making its way through the Duat."

"The Duat?"

"In Egyptian mythology, the soul would enter the Duat, the subterranean sphere, and make its way to the Hall of the Two Truths for judgement."

"Well, I'm sure your mom would pass her judgement," Belinda says with a smile, which I return.

I know Mom would be judged favorably in the afterlife, but Dad on the other hand, I'm not so sure. Would he pass his judgement? He's not a bad person, but I guess I have been judging his shortcomings as a dad very harshly. The thought gives me pause.

The following weekend, I'm stripping the last of the parts off the engine block when Belinda walks into the garage. Her eyes widen when she sees my progress. "You've got a lot done ... you're nearly finished."

"Yeah, need to pull the valves out of the heads."

"Aw ... I can do it ... while you're finishing off the block, if you like?"

I love her enthusiasm and the way she reacts. I smile inwardly as she starts working on the heads.

"When will your dad be home?" she asks. I wonder whether she's trying to avoid bumping into him, and this is almost confirmed when she follows up with the question, "What time do the engine reconditioner's close?"

"At noon. Dad *said* he'd be home in time for me to borrow his truck."

The workshop manual isn't much help at this point, so I close it and throw it on the shelf above the bench that is now littered with car parts.

Once the camshafts out, I find a steel pipe and begin knocking the old bearings out. Belinda has her happy face on while she works on the heads – she's so in her element. I wonder if she enjoys it so much because it's how she bonded with her dad.

"After we drop the block and heads off, I was going to drop past the auto shop. All the parts have come in," I say as I put my tools down.

Belinda's removing the last of the valves as she looks me right in the eye. "Have you ordered a kit for the carburetor?"

I shake my head, wondering why she's asking such a specific question. "Na."

Belinda walks to the open garage door and looks up the driveway. "Your dad's home," she says with an apprehensive look.

I stand by her side. When Dad gets to the house, he turns around and backs up to the edge of the concrete. Belinda and I exchange a nervous glance.

When Dad gets out the truck, he slams the door closed and walks toward us. "Belinda," he says curtly.

"Hi, Mr. Roberts," she says with a half-wave.

We follow him over to the stripped-down block that is still bolted to the engine stand.

He looks it over before handing me the keys to his truck. "Take it easy," he says.

After closing the garage door behind him, Belinda steps in close. "He looks tired," she says softly.

I try to read her face. "Yeah ... I guess."

Loading the block into the back of Dad's truck is a bit of a struggle, but after it's in, we load the heads and prepare to leave. I'm lucky to have Belinda as a friend. This would be near impossible without her help.

I glance over at her as we drive into the city. "Do you want to grab a bite to eat after we do the rounds?"

She smiles. "Yeah, sure."

I'm starting to get the impression she enjoys hanging out with me as much as I do her.

I wonder what she's like when she's with her friends. They are all the type to wear dresses, even in winter, and never have a hair out of place. There has to be a girly side to her I've not seen before, or maybe her friends just accept her for who she is.

Maybe that's why I have so few friends? I should probably try to be more accepting of people – accept Dad for how distant he is, for whatever the reason he's like that.

As we walk in the auto shop, the man that served me the other day calls out, "Kyle. How's it going, buddy?"

I've only met him the once, but I guess spending nearly a thousand dollars on parts makes us friends.

I force a smile. "Hey."

He walks to the end of the counter where a trolley is filled with boxes and shrink-wrapped cardboard packages that I ordered in.

I widen my eyes. "Oh, hell! It's like Christmas."

"You're going to be a busy man," he says.

Belinda sees my wide eyes and smiles. "You didn't think it would be easy, did you?"

I laugh. "No ... not really."

After loading up all the parts, we drop past a takeaway shop and get some fries before driving down to the park. The park is usually so lush and green during summer, but now it is hidden under a white blanket of snow.

We stay in the truck as we sit eating quietly, the aroma of the fries filling the air and the warmth fogging the windscreen.

I look over and notice that there is skin scraped off on Belinda's knuckles and several big scratches on her hands from working on the car. "Do you tell your friends about me ... about working on the car?"

Belinda's clearly taken aback. "Why wouldn't I?"

I shrug. "I don't know."

We sit in silence for a moment.

"What sort of things do you do with your friends ... on weekends?" I ask.

"Most of them live in Denver, so they don't come out here much. I normally meet them there ... go to the cinemas ... go shopping, or whatever."

"Do you like our school?"

"Yeah ... but I feel guilty, though. I think Dad wants me to go to college, but my grades aren't that good. And anyway, I want to follow in his footsteps instead, become a mechanic. I've been wanting to tell him, but I can't pluck up the courage after all the money he's spent on school."

"I know I don't know your dad that well, but I think he'd be proud ... that you want to follow in his footsteps."

Belinda smiles. "Has your dad been helping with your car?"

I shake my head. "No. I guess he doesn't have time."

Belinda frowns and we lock eyes. "Will he?"

The question makes my heart sink; a heart that is now so filled with pain. I often wish I had also died with Mom in the accident. "I had hoped he would, and we'd become closer, but now, I'm not so sure. I don't think anything can bring us closer."

Belinda looks down at the floor of the truck. "I can't imagine my father not helping. But then again, my dad hasn't lost two wives. I can't imagine what your dad's been through."

I'm starting to feel really deflated. "He's been like that for as long as I can remember. There was a time in Egypt when our relationship seemed to improve, but then ..." I stop, not wanting to relive those memories. "I wish I had a dad like yours."

Belinda stares at me with an intense look. Her mouth remains parted, as if she's surprised. She looks like she's choosing her next words carefully. "Have you tried reaching out to him?"

I shake my head, feeling the darkness of depression setting in. I don't know what I'd do without Belinda, I'd be all alone again.

Belinda picks up on my sudden shift in mood and doesn't press the subject. We both sit quietly eating, lost in our thoughts. I know there's always two sides to a story and there must be a reason for why Dad is the way he is. Under that tough, intimidating exterior, I know there is a softer, caring side to him. Maybe one day he'll change. One can only hope.

Belinda and I are sitting together in science class, watching as our teacher prepares for an experiment. It's beyond perfect that Belinda and I are in the same science class, as it's the only subject I'm interested in, and I'm an avid reader on the subject.

Now that Belinda and I are closer, it's the best part of my day.

Mr. Tansley lights a match, which he has attached to a long stick. The class is dead silent. A bowl of black powder is on the table in front of him, and as he lowers the match into the bowl, there's a flash, and a puff of white smoke mushrooms up. He waves his hand, trying to clear the smoke. "Can anyone tell me what the three constituents of black powder are?"

I rarely answer Mr. Tansley's questions, preferring to fly under the radar, but hanging out with Belinda is bringing me out of my shell, and I raise my hand. I'm nervous about answering, but I figure what the hell. "Potassium nitrate, sulfur, and carbon."

"That's correct. Can anyone tell me what each of the chemical's purposes are when used in black powder?"

"Potassium nitrate is an oxidizer, and sulfur and carbon are fuels," I reply.

Mr. Tansley raises his eyebrows. "Very good. Potassium nitrate is an oxidizer, which means it accepts electrons and in turn releases oxygen ..."

I glance over at Belinda. She smiles as she swivels on her stool and lightly punches my leg. I laugh, feeling like a nerd for knowing the answer, but in a good way.

"How did you become interested in chemistry?" she asks.

"Through ancient Egyptian mythology." I chuckle.

Belinda cocks an eyebrow. "Huh?"

"In ancient Egyptian mythology there was a strong celestial component ..." I say, trying to keep my voice down. "About the Sun God – Ra – journeying through the sky ... the stars being gods. I started reading up about how stars are born, live, and die, and how the elements are made in stars. That's how I became interested in chemistry." I can't quite read Belinda's face, but I think she's impressed. "We should ask Mr. Tansley for some ingredients so we can make some black powder at home," I whisper, getting quite excited about the idea; the danger of blowing something up feels thrilling to me.

"What's the difference between black powder and gunpowder?" Belinda asks.

I shrug. "Don't know. I think gunpowder is just more refined ... doesn't produce smoke."

Her eyes suddenly widen as she leans in and whispers, "We could make a cannon."

When the bell rings for end of class, everyone runs for the door as Mr. Tansley packs his gear away. Belinda and I wait for the class to depart before approaching him.

"Kyle, Belinda, what can I do for you?"

I glance over at Belinda and prepare myself. "Can we have some potassium nitrate, sulfur, and carbon? To make some black powered at home."

Mr. Tansley raises his eyebrows and shakes his head ever so slightly as though not quite sure how to answer.

"We won't tell anyone where we got it," I add.

He steps into the back room and gestures for us to follow. He looks up at all the jars containing powders and liquids as though carefully considering the question. He seems to be trying to suppress a smile. I guess he's thrilled that some of his students are showing an interest in chemistry. He then walks to the doorway to make sure we're alone. "All right, but you didn't get it from the school. Okay?"

Belinda and I both agree.

He finds two black film canisters and begins to fill the first one. He looks me in the eye as he fits the gray lid. "I could lose my job for this."

"We won't say a word, sir," I assure him.

He shakes his head while he fills the second canister. "Here," he says, handing me the two film canisters. "You can make your own carbon."

Belinda and I frown, thank him and head for the door.

I stuff the film canisters in my pocket. "So, he's given us potassium nitrate and sulfur, all we need is the carbon to make the black powder, but how do we make carbon?"

Belinda shrugs. "Don't look at me. You're the chemist!"

Chapter 8

Thoth stands in the prow, reading his book, as we journey through the Duat on the Mesektet. Horus controls the steering oar, and Anput sits by Shani's side. There's a tranquil silence over the land, only broken by the sounds of rippling of water. I join the twin goddesses, Isis and Nephthys, as they stand by Atum's side.

"O Isis, if Nephthys is correct, and Tau is the thief of Aya's and Eman's hearts, find him we must."

"Anubis, we shall yield before long," Isis says. "I ask for the Osiris Shani to use akhu, the magic which I bestowed upon her, for thou and Horus to join her, for the three of ye to fly over the land, for this is the land of Heh. Go unto him upon Shu, God of Air, and seek his council, for he may know of the thief whom we seek. On your journey, search for the languid one, Tau. If located, question him."

I bow toward Isis and Nephthys.

As Horus steers us toward land, I go to Shani and hold out my hand. "The Osiris Shani, it is time for you to use akhu. You will transform into a swallow and join Horus and myself. We will fly to Heh, the god that sees all, to seek his council. For Aya's and Eman's hearts must be found and returned."

"O Lord Anubis, I would be honored to join you."

"Do you remember the words from the Book of the Dead, the chapter for transforming into a swallow?" I ask.

"I do," Shani says with an affirmative nod.

Shani and I walk down the gangplank to the shore.

I kneel before Shani. "The Osiris Shani, do not fear, for your ba will be free."

Shani speaks the spell for transforming into that of a swallow. "I am at one with Shu, journeying on his roads. I am the small one who has a home in the Field of Reeds, where the blessed dead dwell. Give power unto my wings so I may go on an errand for Isis. I shall become the small, feathered creature that is as swift as a shadow."

When Shani finishes reciting the spell, her human form shrinks, and she is transformed into that of a swallow – suspended in the air where her chest just was. She flutters her wings in a panic before landing. Standing upon the sandy shore on her twig-like legs, she jumps about, clearly eager to take to the sky.

I too recite my spell and, transformed into a falcon of gold, land by Shani's side. Horus returns to his natural form, a divine falcon, and lands on the shore before us.

"Horus, God of the Sky, will you lead the way? Will you take us to Heh, using your razor-sharp eyes?" I ask.

"I will," replies Horus as he leaps into the air and spreads his wings.

Shani, in her new swallow form, takes to the air with grace, her wings fluttering with exuberance as she follows Horus. I take off and fly ever higher, joining Horus and Shani.

From high up, we can see far, as far as our sharp eyes will allow. We journey along the roads of the sky, until far below, I spot Tau wandering the desert. It's almost as though he doesn't exist, with no one by his side. Some restless souls wander the desert for eternity; others succumb to the permanent watery grave of non-existence. I'm not sure which is worse.

Horus folds his wings in tight and bombs down from the sky. I follow quickly after. Tau looks skyward and runs. Horus' feathers ruffle from the violent air blasting over our bodies as we dive. Horus spreads his wings and extends his talons, threatening to strike.

Tau stops dead in his tracks, and we land in the desert before Tau, who has terror in his eyes.

Shani finally catches up and lands close by my side.

"Tau, why do you run?" Horus asks, his sharp beak gleaming.

"You were chasing me; I was scared," Tau says, breathing heavily.

Horus bounces forward and sinks his sharp talons into the sand. He crooks his neck and stares at Tau intensely with his beady eyes. "What do you know of Aya and Eman?"

"Who?" Tau asks with a puzzled look.

"Aya and Eman entered the Duat of this night, as have you. Their hearts have been stolen. What do you know of it?" Horus asks.

Tau looks at the three of us with obvious rising panic. "I don't know what you're talking about. I am not a thief!"

His assertion is very convincing, but we know better.

"You expect us to believe that it is merely coincidence that you arrive on the same night when two hearts are stolen?" I ask.

"I swear to you," Tau says. "If I stole the hearts of two souls, where are they?" He holds out his empty palms to the sky.

As a God of Embalming, I have the power to see into the heart of a person's ba and see them for who they really are. Looking into Tau's heart, I see a soul bereft of honesty and morality, filled with deceit and villainy, yet with a soul this corrupt and lacking any sense of guilt, I can't be certain he stole the hearts. I look Horus in the eye, silently asking what he wants to do next.

"Tau," Horus says sternly, "we will be keeping an eye on you, for the thief of the hearts *will* be found. You still must pay for past transgressions before this night is out. We will meet again. For that, you have my word." Horus leaps into the air and begins to fly away.

I take one last look at Tau, reading his face. I have no doubt that the thief, whomever it may be, is a master manipulator and knows how not to be caught. I only hope, if Tau is the thief, we can return Aya's and Eman's hearts before it is too late.

Horus and I flap our wings, then glide into the air, as Shani flutters her little wings to keep up with us. Of the many forms one can assume, that of a bird is the most free.

The Lake of Natron appears on the northern akhet. Vast are its waters. We fly over the lake for some time, until I spot a mound of dirt rising from the water like an island. I swoop down, folding my wings in close to my body. The air buffets over my ears as I gain speed. I level out, slow, and land on the mound. Horus lands next to me, and a short while later, Shani lands also. We look out over the water as I've seen Heh do many times before.

"O Lord Anubis, I feel uneasy, as if this place has great importance," Shani says.

"The Osiris Shani, this mound is the birthplace of all ... It is called Benben, the place where Atum created Shu and Tefnut ... where Atum stood and contemplated eternity. The Lake of Natron is where the Great God, Ra, cleansed himself. It is where Anput and I replenish our supplies for embalming."

"O Lord Anubis, I am honored that you would bring me here. That I have had a chance to see the place that comes to me in my dreams."

I bow my head. "We must keep going for we have a great distance to cover, and Atum's bark must continue."

After leaving Benben, we fly for some time before the northern bank of the Lake of Natron comes into view.

Far away is he, but the giant Heh can be seen sitting at the edge of the water. He stares into the lake, deep in thought. We are flying higher than any mast, higher than any tree, and yet when Heh stands, it is only his shoulders we align to. His body is that of water, his skin rippled like the lake. In one hand, he holds a palm stem filled with notches, and at the base of the stem is a solid-gold shen-sign. In his hair he wears a smaller palm stem and around his neck, a wide mantel.

As we approach, he holds his hand out and we land upon his watery palm. It is as though we are standing on water. Shani's little swallow head twitches as her eyes dart over Heh, taking in the grandeur of his existence.

"O Lord Heh, God of Eternity, we have come in need of your help," Horus says.

"Horus, Anubis, and the Osiris Shani—" When Heh speaks, his bellowing voice crashes through the air like a wave. "—I was around at the birth of all matter and will be around at its end. What is it that you seek?"

"O Lord Heh, we are seeking the thief of Aya's and Eman's hearts," Horus says. "We have questioned the languid one, Tau, but have arrived no closer to discovering the truth."

"You are wise to seek my council. You will find no truth in Tau, only lies. Why Aya and Eman, you should ask yourself, and what is the purpose of such an abomination? The answers to these questions will lead you to the thief."

"O Lord Heh," Horus says, "we thank you, and on behalf of my father, Osiris thanks you."

Heh bows his head. "There is one more thing you should know. Marks on the shore of the Lake of Natron, I have seen. Someone has stolen clay from behind my back."

More theft. It seems unlikely that Tau could be behind it, for if he stole the clay, we would have seen him with it.

"O Lord Heh," I say. "The theft of the hearts, the theft of the clay, what purpose could these two things have?"

Heh shakes his head. "Leave me to contemplate that question, but I fear the answer you will not like, for stealing clay from the Lake of Natron would take great deceit."

"O Lord Heh, thank you for sharing your knowledge," I say. "It may indeed save Aya's and Eman's bas."

Heh bows his head.

Horus, Shani, and I take to the skies again.

When the Mesektet is once more in view, we swoop down from high in the sky and land on the shore, transforming back into our normal forms: Horus, a falcon-headed man; Shani, a woman; and me, a man with the head of a jackal.

Isis is standing at the gunwale. "Anubis, what of Heh? What words of wisdom did he share?"

"O Isis," I say to my mother, "Heh suggested not seeking the thief, but instead, seeking the truth as to why Aya and Eman have be targeted. He also suggests we seek the truth as to the purpose of such theft."

Isis looks into Horus' eyes and with pinched eyebrows thinks aloud. "Heh is indeed wise."

"There is more," I add. "Someone has stolen clay from the Lake of Natron. For what could the clay be used?"

"Many things," Isis replies, "tablets, Canopic jars, to create the forms of all manner of creature. If the words the thief knows, life can be breathed into clay forms of people or creatures. What of Tau, did thou find him on your travels?"

"We did," I reply, "but he did not know of Aya and Eman. In his possession were neither hearts nor clay. I believe he likely stole the hearts, but his heart is so filled therewith deceit and villainy, it makes it hard for me to be sure. A life so filled with lie upon lie makes questions fruitless."

Isis shakes her head. "We must continue, for Atum cannot wait. We must learn the answers to these questions on our journey, and as Heh says, it will lead us to the corrupt ones, and stopped they will be."

Chapter 9

It's Saturday morning, and after dropping Dad off at work, I drive to the cemetery. The thought of visiting Mom's grave has been heavy on my mind for over a month. I park and sit in Dad's truck, looking out over the tombstones for a moment before getting out. Snow crunches beneath my feet, and my breath mists the air. Surrounded by tombstones and snow-blanketed gardens, I visit my birth mom's grave first. It's in an older part of the cemetery where few people now visit. I kneel in front of her tombstone and read the inscription as I often do, feeling a pang of sadness when I read the dates. She was only twenty-five when she passed.

I've always felt incredibly guilty for being born, as if she paid for my birth with her life. I picture her face as it is in the old, faded photo that sits on my nightstand. My wavy hair I get from Dad, but my eyes are from her. I wish I knew more about her.

Dad's heart has probably turned to stone now after losing two wives. It's a wonder he can function at all.

As I walk toward the newer part of the cemetery where Mom's grave is, I try to put myself in his shoes. I can now understand why he would want to come here on his own time – he's probably scared he'll break down in front of me. However, I don't understand why we both have to suffer in silence. You'd think losing Mom would bring us closer, but it's like she was the bridge between us, and now she's gone, we're further apart than ever before.

I kneel in front of Mom's tombstone. She was only thirty-eight years old. A tear crawls down my cheek as though it's being frozen in its tracks. I wipe it away and empty my lungs – there's a heavy pain in my chest. *Why? Why was she stolen from me?*

I wish it was Dad that died instead.

"I miss you so much ... I wish I was with you."

I reach out to brush the snow off Mom's tombstone, and on contact, I freeze as a vision overtakes my senses ...

Walking through dark hallways, I reach out and run my fingers over the rough face of the limestone walls. Warm air courses past. I peer around the corner to another hallway, continuing forward.

The sound of deep breathing is carried on the draft, like monstrous lungs rasping the air. The putrid smell of rotting flesh wafts past. My heart quickens. I'm torn between wanting to discover the source and running for my life. I'm not alone, but who else is in here? What else is in here?

I recognize the face as she prowls around the corner – its Ammit, Swallower of the Dead. Her giant hippopotamus hindquarters anchor her to the floor; her lion front paws and claws scratch at the limestone floor, and her crocodile head hisses as she opens her jaws and flashes an armory of teeth.

I step back, my heart pounding, and then run. The sound of sharp claws and monstrous footsteps chase after me. I hurriedly retrace my steps, looking for

an exit, but the hallway is a dead end.
My back is against the wall. Ammit
rounds the last corner then slows to a
walk, hissing and drooling as she
moves. With no escape, my adrenaline
rages.

Ammit runs toward me, opening her
jaws wide.

I fall back in fright, my legs and arms flailing to get away from Mom's tombstone. Sitting in the snow, propped up on my hands, my gasps mist the air over and over. I spring to my feet and dust the snow off. *What was that? Was that the Duat? It must be.*

The weighing of the heart ceremony would be in a place like that, with the limestone walls. In the ceremony, it is Ammit who watches over the souls, ready to devour those hearts that are heavier than the feather of Maat. Why was that vision so different to the others? Why *that* vision, and not those where I am aboard the Mesektet like the others? I wonder if touching Mom's tombstone allows me to see into the Duat.

"I wish I was with you, Mom, on your journey through the Duat," I whimper, not willing to touch her tombstone again.

I have to find something to explain all of this before it pushes me over the edge. I have so many questions, like why am *I* Anubis in my visions?

I now know they're not nightmares, as the last couple of visions came to me during the day while awake. The visions now seem to come and go with no discernible splice into reality. I'm not even sure what's real anymore.

Walking back to the truck, my mind goes into overdrive and my emotions are all jumbled. I climb in through the driver's side door and take a deep breath, on the verge of breaking into tears. I slam the door and just sit awhile, trying to clear my mind. The tombstones in the bleak winter are such a solemn scene.

I remember Uncle Tim telling me once that if you find yourself in a deep hole that you can't get out of, the first thing you should do is stop digging. But I can't, that's not an option. I have to know what my visions mean.

First, I drive to the engine reconditioners to pick up my engine block and heads, then I drive into the city to return my book on delusions. I also plan to look for any other books at the library that might provide answers. I park in the largely empty carpark and climb out.

Inside, the air is warm. There are umbrellas and coats hanging in the foyer. I approach the returns counter and slide my book across the counter.

The librarian studies the cover intensely. "Did you find what you were looking for?"

"No, but thank you," I say, then race away before she can ask any more questions. Although most of that book was over my head, I'm sure my visions aren't religious delusions.

I head toward the shelves with ancient Egyptian mythology books and scan the spines. I've probably read half of them by now, but I spot one called *The Egyptian Book of the Dead*. The cover has Ani and Tut standing in adoration before Osiris in mummiform. *Score.* I remember Mom bringing home a copy of this book three or so years ago when we were still living in Cairo. I open it and flick through to the vignettes and hieroglyphs. If I can't find the answers I'm looking for in this book, I won't find them at all. I reminisce about Mom as I look at the beautiful artwork, which makes me even more depressed. The wish of having died in the accident returns to the fore of my mind.

It's early Sunday morning and I'm freezing on the walk down to Belinda's. I woke at four in the morning and couldn't get back to sleep, so spent the morning reading *The Egyptian Book of the Dead*. I'm hoping I'm not too early.

I'm relieved when Belinda opens her front door with no visible frustration in her face.

Warren's in his armchair watching the television when I enter.

"How's your rebuild going?" he asks when he sees me.

After filling him in, he offers to help in any way he can, which I appreciate greatly.

Belinda points toward her bedroom with her head, and I follow her down the hall. It's the first time I've been in her room, and I'm not entirely surprised to see the mix of styles that represent the different parts of her personality. The walls are covered with posters of heavy metal bands and cars, and the shelves are filled with jewelry boxes and cheap ceramic figurines of ballerinas. Hanging on the wall is what looks like a vintage blacksmith hammer –that, or a medieval mallet for caving in skulls.

I look Belinda in the eye as I pull the ready-made copper bomb from my pocket.

Her eyes widen. "What the hell is that? Did you figure out how to make carbon?"

I nod. "I just crushed up some charcoal. Charcoal's essentially just carbon; I'm guessing that's why Mr. Tansley told us to make our own. I mixed some up and tested it ... it burns quite well."

Belinda looks like she's trying to read my face. "Oh ... okay. I was looking forward to building a cannon, but if you want, we can take it down to the lake to set it off."

"Yeah, okay. I've got matches."

I glance over at Belinda as we traipse through the snow. I can't wait for summer, I'm sick of the snow. It would be so nice to come down to the water and swim and lie around in the sun. I can't help but hope that by then we'll be more than just friends.

"Where should we put it?" Belinda asks when we make it to the water's edge.

"I don't know ... we should probably be well clear of it." I look around and point to a large boulder we could use as a shield. I place the copper bomb at the base and suggest that we go further up the hill.

Belinda nods and takes off, while I wait a few moments before lighting the wick. I run after her, my adrenaline coursing.

When I reach the top of the hill, I hunker down beside Belinda in the snow, and we both sit, grimacing, unable to see the wick from our position. The suspense is excruciating.

A second later there's a solid boom and the sound of torn metal screeching through the air. The sulfuric smell of burned black powder fills the air. We both laugh wildly.

"That was awesome," I say between fits of laughter. "I didn't think it would work that well."

Belinda punches me on the shoulder. "Aw ... you're mad!"

She's probably right, but not in a good way. The momentary exhilaration I felt from the explosion pushes the tide of depression back, and now the moment of elation has passed, the tide comes flooding back in. My thoughts are consumed by my visions, and I wonder if they do indeed make me "mad." I hate being so depressed all the time.

I don't know how long it's been since I laughed like that, and I'm aching for that feeling again as I sit by her side. Belinda's face is still glowing with excitement. I love her enthusiasm for life and wish I was more like her. I try to match her excitement but can't seem to muster enough to be convincing.

Belinda drops her smile and frowns. "What's wrong?"

I look her in the eyes, deadpan, and shake my head. I wish I could tell her everything: about my depression, my visions, and about the deep feelings I have for her. But she'd probably run for the hills if she knew. I don't think I could take losing her too.

Belinda bumps her shoulder against mine. Her face hardens as she looks me in the eye. "What are you thinking about?"

"I think Mom would have liked you," I say, glancing up at her.

"Did you end up visiting her grave yesterday morning?"

I nod.

She studies my face intensely for a moment before asking, "When did you make the copper bomb?"

"Yesterday afternoon."

Belinda frowns, clearly deep in thought, before looking out over the water. I admire her beautiful face and picture what it would be like to kiss her delicate lips; even the thought of it makes my heart race.

I walk into William's building after school and find him standing behind the counter, rifling through his briefcase.

A small gold crucifix hangs from a chain around his neck that I hadn't noticed before.

"Hi, Kyle," he says, finally finding what he was looking for.

"Hi," I say, following him down the hall.

As we enter the room, he hands me a flier from the Denver Museum. It has a photo of a giant statue of Anubis on it and all the details of an ancient Egypt exhibition that is coming up.

"I saw this the other day and thought of you?" he says.

I look down at the flier, then up at him, immediately thinking of the double meaning it holds if he knew I was having visions of being Anubis.

"Thank you," I say as I plonk myself onto the couch. "That looks great. I'll definitely be going to that one."

"How have you been doing?" William asks.

"Okay," I reply, not really wanting to talk about everything that has been going on.

William sits on the couch over from me, holding my file in his hand. "How have the antidepressants been going? Have you been taking them?"

I nod. "They make my legs twitch when I'm trying to fall asleep."

"Have they been helping your mood at all?"

"No. My depression's getting worse, and I'm struggling to get a good night's sleep. Several times a week I don't fall asleep until about two am."

"Could we try another antidepressant then?" William asks.

I nod again, though I'm not ecstatic by this "just try" approach, which seems random. I don't know why, but William seems even older than I remembered. The permanent heavy lines on his forehead give new meaning to a furrowed brow. He's like an old leather-bound book with many pages.

"Any thoughts of self-harm?"

"From time to time," I reply solemnly. Not wanting to talk about it, I change the subject, but not thinking, I blurt out, "I made a copper bomb the other day. Belinda and I let it off behind her place."

William smiles, frowning with concern. "Sounds like fun."

I nod. "I've become friends with Belinda now."

"Oh yeah. That's great. Making friends is a really important step in overcoming depression. It can take hundreds, if not thousands, of hours to make new friends, and having those ties with the community can go a long way."

I can attest to that. Whenever I'm around Belinda, I usually feel better.

William scratches his beard and adds, "If you've been treated badly or, if like you, have a family member or friend leave unexpectedly, it can cause you to retreat from society, to stop trying to make new friends. It can create a negative feedback loop where you retreat more; you become more depressed, and it becomes harder for others to want to be around you. When you become extremely lonely and disconnected, you become hypervigilant, suspicious of others, and sometimes oversensitive. So that's a really good first step ... making new friends."

"She's a bit of a tomboy and has been helping me rebuild my Mustang's engine."

William raises his eyebrows. "That's excellent ... really! Beating loneliness isn't just about surrounding yourself with people. You can go into a big city and still experience loneliness while being completely surrounded by people. You need to share something that matters to both of you, so her helping you rebuild the engine is a great thing to share. It should bring the two of you closer. Forming a close relationship with Belinda will help at school too. You still mightn't like your classmates, but you likely won't hate them as much if that feeling of alienation subsides."

I smile, picturing Belinda covered in grease and dirt.

"You know that's the first time I've seen you smile," William says, giving me a curious look.

I drop the smile immediately.

"You're obviously enjoying her company."

I think about the good times we have shared and the meaningful conversations we've had. "Yeah. I love being around her."

"I didn't know you had a Mustang."

"Yeah. I bought it off my uncle."

"Has your dad been helping at all?"

I shake my head, immediately feeling awful from the lost hope that he would help and that we'd become closer. "No."

"What sort of car does your dad drive?"

I frown. *Why should that matter?* "Just an old pick-up truck. It's as old as my Mustang. It's one of the few things I actually admire about him."

William cocks his head to one side. "What's that?"

"He doesn't buy crap for the sake of buying crap. Our house is really old as well."

"Your dad sounds like a wise man. People that buy things just to show them off, which are extrinsic values, are often the most unhappy. Extrinsic values can definitely contribute to depression."

William puts his pen down and looks at me intensely, as if what he has to say is really important. "But people that value intrinsic things, experiences such as rebuilding a car engine or doing charity work, not because it will impress your friends or raise your status, but simply because you enjoy doing it and you want to learn something new or help others, are the people that more often than not find happiness. However, a caveat I would add to that is that just because someone buys a fancy car, it doesn't necessarily make it an extrinsic value. They may have simply bought that car for the safety features and are putting their kid's safety first."

"Oh." I hadn't really thought of it like that. I guess I'm guilty of tarring everyone at my school with the same brush. "Then why am I so depressed then?"

"It takes time for those things to take effect. You only lost your mother, what, six weeks ago, and you've only just made friends with Belinda and found joy in working on your car. Your dad sounds like a moral man. He's done well to bring you up with those same values."

I know Dad's not a bad person, he'll never win a father of the year award, but what William is saying is true. "Why do I have such a bad relationship with Dad then?"

"Has it always been bad?"

"It's never been great, but I do remember it getting worse about a year before we left Egypt."

"That's around the same time your friend Ramsi left?"

I shift my weight to get comfortable and nod.

"Did anything else happen around that same time?"

Thinking back to that time, I navigate my way around some of my horrifying memories. I don't need any more reasons to feel depressed – but I decide to share my "version" of the things that happened then. "I don't know ... Ramsi and his dad left at the same time the plant shut down. There was a malfunction with the brick press, and the whole plant had to shut down for a day or two while they fixed it. Maybe Ramsi's dad stuffed up and was fired for breaking the press."

William's busy taking notes, so I continue, "I only worked there for a couple of weeks after the plant reopened. I remember Dad being excited about me being there, showing me the ins and outs of the plant and why they did things the way they did. But after I stopped working there, that spark vanished, and we stopped talking to each other."

"Do you think he wanted you to work at the plant once you finished school?"

I look off into the distance, pondering this. "I think he used to."

"When the brick plant shut down, do you remember what emotions you were feeling at the time? Anger? Sadness? Depression?"

"Do you ever think about the elements that make up your body?"

William frowns. "Can't say I do."

"The elements that make up your body were created billions of years ago in a star ... oxygen, carbon, nitrogen, iron ... they've traveled across the face of the Earth in one form or another ... as a bird, a tree, only to find their way to you. Do you think that's why people are materialistic, that they're afraid of death and that holding onto material things is an extension of holding onto their material bodies?"

William frowns even harder. "Are you afraid of death?" he asks, to which I shake my head. He adds with a cheeky smile breaking through, "Is that why you're not materialistic?"

I chuckle. "Touché."

He grins and makes more notes. "Have you tried speaking to your dad? Reaching out?"

I shake my head, my smile vanishing.

"You should," he says in a sincere voice. "Keep in mind ... he's likely hurting as much as you. Maybe the two of you could go to the exhibition together."

I nod, picking up the flier and reading it. "I guess it couldn't hurt to ask."

"I read the back of the flier, what's the Book of the Dead?" he asks, sounding genuinely interested.

"The Book of the Dead was a papyrus that was buried with the dead to help them through the Duat," I explain. "It contained hymns, spells, and lots of vignettes of the expansive pantheon of deities and their many forms."

"What's the Duat?"

"The ancient Egyptians believed the Earth was flat, and at the junction between the subterranean sphere, the celestial sphere, and the ends of the Earth were the akhets," I say. Talking about the Duat is getting me excited about the exhibition, so I keep going. It must be the most I've ever spoken in one of our sessions. "Under the Earth, the subterranean sphere, there was the land called the Duat where a river flowed. Ra would die each evening, enter the Duat at the western akhet, travel on his bark from west to east, and then be reborn each morning at the eastern akhet."

"What's a bark?"

"It's a kind of boat."

William smiles. "You know your whole demeanor changed when you started talking about the Duat. You're obviously very passionate about it."

I smile again, thinking about Mom, but when my mind ventures back to the visions I've been having, the feeling that I'm drowning in a flood of darkness and sorrow takes over again. I don't know whether reading *The Egyptian Book of the Dead* has been helping or is just making things worse.

William gives me a focused look and clears his expression. "What were you just thinking about?"

I shake my head, glancing up at him; I guess I must have pulled a face.

"Do you think your mom's in the Duat?" he asks. I can see what he's doing – asking me more questions to get me talking again.

"Yeah. I believe that Mom's soul is in the Duat, and she's making her way to the east."

"What happens when a soul makes it to the east?"

"If they're innocent, they can enter the Field of Reeds, which is sort of like heaven. From there they can go-forth-by-day."

"What?" He shakes his head in confusion.

"The ancient Egyptians believed that when you reached the Field of Reeds, your soul could temporarily leave the Duat and reenter your body and you could walk about on Earth. That's why they preserved their bodies."

"Oh. I get it. So, all those movies where mummies are walking around are reflecting that thinking."

"Sort of. Most movies inaccurately depict mummies, though. They're not bad things at all. When you 'go-forth-by-day' it wasn't as an evil mummy, it was as a vindicated, innocent person getting to live with their loved ones again on Earth. After which, if you were truly blessed, you could be reunited with your ka, your life force, and join the gods in the celestial sphere as an akh."

William laughs. "Sounds complicated."

I laugh too. *I guess it is.*

"Well, let me know if you start seeing your mom walking around the house," he says, giving me a wink.

I smile back at him. While my visions have been terrifying, especially when I touched Mom's tombstone, I hope one day they will eventually be pleasant. Maybe one day I will even get to see Mom go-forth-by-day.

I spend the next morning cleaning down the Mustang's engine block and fitting it to Warren's engine stand. I unpack the camshaft's bearings and wipe the oil off them. I read through the workshop manual again, but there isn't much information on how to insert them. So, I improvise, finding an old broomstick, cut a few feet off the end and use the dowel to tap the first bearing into place. A couple minutes later, all the bearings are in. *Not too bad, if I do say so myself.*

A car pulls up outside and I walk to the edge of the concrete to see it's Craig.

"Hey, did you get your braces off?"

He grins like a Cheshire cat, showing off his clean, newly straightened teeth. "Yeah. Good, right?"

He's all dressed up like he has a hot date or something, but knowing him, he's probably just going to walk around town, bored shitless like he usually is. I point toward the garage with my head, and he follows.

"I was just going to insert the camshaft ... want to help?"

"Not really," he replies unenthusiastically. "I'm going into town. Did you want to come?"

I shake my head, pointing at my engine. "I've got too much work to do."

He looks down at the ground, rejected. We both stand silent for a moment before he says, "All right then ... I'll see you at school."

"See ya." I watch him walk back to his car. In hindsight, I don't know why I asked if he'd like to help; I can't picture him getting his hands dirty.

I lube up the camshaft bearings with some engine oil and insert the camshaft. With the timing gear fitted, I try turning it by hand, but it won't budge. *Damn it.* That's not good. I grab hold of the timing gear with both hands, and it turns a bit before locking up. *Crap. What am I doing?* Dad was right. What do I know about engines?

The very first step in rebuilding the engine is a failure. An overwhelming sense of depression – hopelessness and worthlessness – floods my body. I sit on the steps between the house and garage and rub my forehead, feeling like a complete idiot. I wish I was with Mom in the Duat right now instead of here in the mundane world.

I stare at the engine a while before getting up. The bench is covered with car parts and tools, and I'm completely overwhelmed. *Now what?*

Both Belinda and William have encouraged me to reach out to Dad, and it feels like this is the right time to do it, so I head inside to see if he can help. He's sitting at the dining table reading the paper. After he gave me such a hard time about buying the Mustang, I'm nervous thinking about asking him for help, and I spend some time warming my hands in front of the fire before I summon the courage to speak up.

Dad looks up, reading my face. "What?"

I fill him in on the situation with the engine, how I'm struggling with the camshaft. As I speak, I try to read his face. It's cold, emotionless.

"Just get a flathead screwdriver and scrap some bearing material off, it's pretty soft."

What the hell? Maybe he knows more about engines than I thought. But that advice can't be right. It sounds too crude. I stare at him for a short while – he's gone back to reading his paper – before heading back to the garage.

Almost as if I telepathically summoned them, I hear Belinda's and Warren's voices outside. I look out the garage door, relieved, as if all the weight of my earlier thoughts has lifted.

"Hi, Kyle, how's it going?" Warren says, hobbling into the garage.

"Good thanks."

It's a lie, but I guess the social convention is that you always say you're good, even when you're depressed as all hell. Asking people how they are seems so futile – you never get the truth.

Belinda gives me a big smile, and I try hard to return it.

Almost with clairvoyance, Warren reaches out and tries to turn the camshaft, but it doesn't budge. He then looks at me with wide eyes.

"I don't know what I'm doing," I say. "I just fitted the bearings, camshaft, and timing gear. I used engine oil, but it won't turn."

"Let's have a look," Warren says, reaching out this time with both hands. He tries turning the camshaft by the timing gear again and it still doesn't move. "Yeah ... that's not good. How did you put the bearings in?"

"I just tapped them in with a wooden dowel."

"You know there's a special tool for fitting camshaft bearings?"

"Oh." My heart sinks and I shake my head. "I don't know what I'm doing."

Warren gives me a sympathetic look. "Don't be so hard on yourself. You don't know what you don't know. I have a buddy in town that has the proper tool, how about I take the engine block over to him and he can fit some new bearings?"

"That would be great. Thank you," I reply. "I'm questioning whether I should even be attempting to rebuild the engine myself. I'm not really getting anywhere."

Warren shakes his head. "You'll get there, son. Don't give up. I'm just down the road if you ever get stuck."

He gives me some pointers on some of the other things that aren't covered in the workshop manual, and then Belinda and I load the block into the back of his truck.

I wish Dad was more like Warren. Once again, my friends' dads are better fathers to me than my own. I don't remember the last time Dad helped me with anything.

Belinda decides to stay with me to help, and we wave goodbye to Warren. When he has left, she turns to me and asks enthusiastically, "So, what are we working on?"

My mood instantly lifts. Her beautiful face and spirit warm my heart.

"I thought we could start fitting the valves. Sound good?"

She punches me lightly on the shoulder, a move I find more endearing each time she does it, and says, "Awesome, I love working on the heads."

I can't wipe the smile off my face as we unpack all the new valves, springs, and collets from the pile of parts I picked up from the auto shop the other day. The heads are all shiny from where they've been machined, and my confidence is renewed. With Belinda by my side, I feel like I could get this done.

She gives me a cheeky smile as she gets to work. "You know ... when you get the Mustang running again, you've gotta take me for a drive."

"I know," I reply, feeling enlivened at the thought. This must mean that she expects we'll still be hanging out in the future. I hope we can be more than just friends, that I can take her out on a date.

Chapter 10

Shani stares at the deck as we journey eastward. She looks troubled by something.

"What is it, the Osiris Shani?" I say, taking her hand.

"Tau won't pass his judgement, will he?" she asks.

"Even if he didn't steal the hearts or the clay from the Lake of Natron, he will certainly fail his judgement based on his transgressions in the mundane world."

"O Lord Anubis, I know we've discussed it, and that I shouldn't believe that taking an apple from my friends' house without asking is stealing, but when we get to the Hall of the Two Truths ... I can't help feeling guilt in my heart for my actions in the mundane world."

"The Osiris Shani, beware. For this guilt can affect the weighing of your heart. If your heart is found heavier than the feather of Maat, it will be eaten by Ammit and you will wander restless for eternity. Absolve yourself of this guilt, you must, but do not worry, for there is time."

Shani looks me in the eye. "I wouldn't consider it stealing if a friend stole an apple from *my* house, but shouldn't the victim's beliefs be more important? What if my friend's parents considered it stealing?"

I shake my head. "You already know the answer. You have it in you to reconcile this feeling of guilt."

"When it becomes time to declare my innocence in the Hall of the Two Truths, I wish to say I am innocent, but ..."

"The Osiris Shani, life is rarely absolute, it is fluid. You have already expressed that you would not consider it stealing. You cannot know what others thought of that act, you can only know in your heart whether you lived a true life."

Shani clearly thinks on my words. "I understand," she says, and a smile breaks through her gloomy expression.

I run my hand down the back of her head and rest it on her shoulder to comfort her. Then I leave her to be with her thoughts, joining my soulmate Anput by the gunwale.

"Anubis, what of the Osiris Shani? She looks troubled," Anput says, taking my hand.

"She will be okay," I say. "She is frightened for her heart, that it may be forfeited at the weighing ceremony."

Anput and I look into each other's eyes, into each other's souls.

The desert becomes rocky, and the river narrows, marking the extent of Sokar's territory. Sokar, Lord of Rosetjau, is a god of the necropolis, like Anput and I, but that is where our similarities end. For Sokar lies down with those corrupt ones, Apophis and Seth; he lives on what is putrid and stands in Atum's path nightly.

Shani joins us at the gunwale as the Mesektet speeds forward. We watch the rocky walls of the ravine rush past. The darkest hours of the Duat are at hand. These are the hours when all could be lost.

Sokar, in the form of a falcon, flies overhead, spying on us upon our arrival.

Isis and Nephthys, the twin goddesses, each place a hand on the timber plinth, beside Atum's ram-headed mummiform body. They will guard the Great God with their bas.

Before too long, the ravine opens, and the waters slow. A vast desert and rolling sand dunes can be seen in the distance. No reeds grow here, for Sokar has drained the life of everything – there are tombs and tombstones all around. I can see why some people would call this place Rosetjau, the gateway to the Underworld. I have no doubt Sokar has secret portals here to the mundane world that only he knows about.

Shani points to the land. Amongst the tombstones, Tau is still wandering aimlessly. If he is the thief of Aya's and Eman's hearts and the clay from the Lake of Natron, I cannot conceive of what he has done with them, or for what purpose they serve.

Sokar soars upon the air, circling above Tau, and then, without notice, swoops with his talons outstretched. Tau runs and hides behind a tomb, cowering in fear briefly, before making a break for it. Sokar swoops again, this time snatching Tau in his talons and carrying him skyward. He flies higher and higher until he and Tau are out of sight.

Shani looks up, afraid. She is still carrying her burden of guilt, and I can tell she is worrying that her fate may be that of Tau's. Although she doesn't see it, I know her heart is pure, without equal, and incomparable to Tau's. But before she can reach her judgement, there are many things that could destroy her ba – to cause her to die a second death. I hope she survives these hours of the night, for my heart would bloom with warmth to see her reach the Field of Reeds.

"The Osiris Shani, are you prepared to protect Atum and the Mesektet?" I ask.

"O Lord Anubis, I am."

"A crocodile, you will transform into, when the time is at hand."

Shani bows. "Do all souls die a second death if they are destroyed in the Duat?"

"Most do; however, bas that have been damned, having had their hearts eaten by Ammit, Swallower of the Dead, will wander the Duat restless for eternity. Only the waters of Nun or the Island of Fire can destroy all that remains."

From his position at the steering oar, Horus points to the northern akhet with his free hand. "Anubis, Anput, prepare to disembark."

We look to the northern akhet, where, far away, a great dust storm is building.

"O Lord Anubis, what is that?" Shani asks.

"The Osiris Shani, they are the Sands of the Necropolis. Sokar's army of the damned: rotten corpses brought back to life for this hour of the night by Sokar, leaching off the presence of the Great God, Atum, as he breathes life into everything."

Shani gasps. "Will they attack the bark? Do they mean Atum harm?"

I place my hand on her shoulder. "Indeed. But fear not, for we are with Isis, Goddess of Magic and Spells. Naught can match her powers."

Isis leaves Atum's side and joins us at the gunwale. "Anubis, Anput, the Osiris Shani, the Sands of the Necropolis must not be allowed to fill the Mesektet. Stopped upon shore, they must be."

The gangplank is extended, and we disembark.

"Anubis, my soulmate, I fear for your ba." Anput reaches out a hand.

I hold her hand in mine. "Anput, I will assume many forms, as should you. Together we will fight off the encroachment of Sokar's army." I clench my other hand around my was scepter in anticipation of the coming battle.

Anput bows, acknowledging my plan.

"The Osiris Shani, now is the time to use akhu to transform into a crocodile," I say.

Shani bows and recites the spell: "I am the jackal-like serpent that lurks at the shore. I am the mighty barbed beast that eats what he steals. Give power unto my jaws, give power unto my tail, so I may defeat Ra's enemies, for

I am in his entourage. I shall become like Sobek, the Great Crocodile of the Nile."

Shani's ba transforms into a crocodile. Now on all fours, she waddles forward, leaving a snake-like trail in the sand. She waits there with great anticipation. Her jaws are clenched, her newly formed teeth protruding like alarming rows of broken glass. Sokar's army of the damned, with her impenetrable gray scaly skin, will meet its match in Shani's new form.

Sokar soars high above, preceding the great storm as it nears. White lightning lights up the orange-brown dust storm, before crashing sporadically to the ground. Thunder rolls across the sky to the backdrop of supercharged electricity crackling.

Sokar swoops down, his feathers ruffling and wings tucked tight. Before crashing into the ground, he spreads his wings wide and transforms into his usual form: a falcon-headed mummy. As his feet hit the ground, the Sands of the Necropolis fall out of the sky. The sudden downpour of sand sounds just like rain but is then followed by silence.

As the dust settles, the revenant army of the damned can be seen. Led by Sokar, the bas of thousands march toward us. Little more than decayed skeletons and mummy bandages, they are armed with axes, spears, and knives.

Shani hisses and flashes her serrated teeth. I clench my was scepter tight and glance over at Anput, giving her a nod, and we step forward.

We step outside of our first forms, creating second forms of ourselves, identical to the first. We then step sideways, creating two more. We repeat and repeat until there are hundreds of our forms. An army comprising of myself and Anput, each holding a was scepter, ready for battle. We march forward.

Leading his army of the damned, Sokar runs toward me.

As we meet, our was scepters crash together, locking in a battle of strength and will. Sokar pushes me back, and I'm tripped by one of his soldiers, who is kneeling on all fours behind me. My was scepter flies out of my hand as I land on my back. I grab the soldier and rip his head off in one quick movement; it turns to dust in my hand. The rest of his skeletal body disintegrates and falls to the ground.

Sokar lunges at me once more, and I grab his was scepter with both hands. We struggle until I finally pry it from his hands, using all my strength to knock him to the ground.

The army of the damned keeps coming, still numbering in the hundreds, but I hear Isis behind me reciting one of her most powerful forms of akhu – that of which will divide the duality of good and evil, turning our enemy unto dust.

When Sokar hears the words of Isis, his falcon eyes widen. He knows what is coming next and transforms into a full falcon and takes to the sky. Flying higher and higher, he leaves his own army to their fate.

One of the damned comes at me swinging a craggy-edged axe covered in rust. He's a monster – powerful swings of his axe threatening my very survival. This nightly battle to see Atum through the Duat is one we cannot lose, so I transform into my most powerful form: that of a shadowy mass, a black tempestuous storm cloud with ribbon-like tentacles for wings.

As I fly through the air, the damned soldiers' eyes flare in terror. In this form, I am able to permeate any object, and I invade his body. I expand my mass, growing larger and larger. The damned soldier's body spasms, thrashing about before exploding in a cloud of dust.

I transform back into my normal form and land on the sandy ground. I pick up my was scepter and continue to do battle.

On one side of me, Shani opens her jaws, exposing rows of sharp teeth, before ambushing another damned ba and tearing him limb from limb.

Meanwhile, on the other side, Anput sinks her was scepter into the empty chest cavity of a damned ba and wrenches it sideways. The bones and mummy bandages turn to dust and fall upon the desert sands.

I hear Isis still chanting behind me and know she needs more time, so I find my next opponent. I drive my was scepter into the knee of one of the damned, breaking his leg in two. As he hits the ground, I stand over him, raise my was scepter high and plunge it into his ribcage. His maggoty face looks up, eyeballs and flesh hanging from bones before turning to dust and falling on the ground in a pile.

Isis brings her hands together and a bright blue light explodes outward in a shock wave, expanding faster and faster. Many of Sokar's army run, but it's too late. The shock wave hits the mummy's bandaged skeletal forms, turning them to dust.

And like that, Sokar's army has been vanquished, with cascades of dust falling upon the desert sands.

Anput and I merge our multiple forms until there's only ourselves as individuals again. Shani retakes her form of a woman.

"The Osiris Shani, you have seen to Isis' will and have risked dying a second death," I say. "We welcome your courage in Atum's entourage."

"O Lord Anubis, I am honored to have been of help."

Anput and I take Shani's hands and walk back to the Mesektet. Isis is standing at the gunwale. She smiles and I return it, for I know that while the darkest hour of the night is still ahead, we have cleared the way for Atum, and he will be reborn again soon.

Chapter 11

It's early Saturday morning. As I sit and eat my breakfast, I'm stressing about visiting Mom's grave but am also excited. At least after dropping Dad off at work, I'll be going there alone. If I have another vision, I can keep it to myself. After washing up my bowl and placing it in the dish drainer, I find a newspaper in the trash. *That's weird.* Dad normally keeps all papers to light the fire.

I pull it from the trash and an article at the bottom of the front cover immediately catches my eye. It reads: *Conifer Crescent Accident Claims Second Life – truck driver commits suicide.* I gasp and reach out for the kitchen bench as I drop onto a stool. I can't believe this, although I can relate. I study the photo of the driver. He's standing in front of his truck, smiling. The picture of the truck immediately brings flashbacks. My eye's tear up and I swallow hard, instantly feeling the shadow of depression enveloping me. *This world is so cruel.* That poor family. Mom would be heartbroken.

After reading the article, I put the paper back in the trash, trying to place it exactly how I found it. I wonder if Dad was trying to protect me by throwing it out instead of putting it with the other papers by the fireplace.

"You ready?" he asks, walking out from his room.

I nod, clearing any emotions from my face, and we walk out to the garage. I was looking forward to visiting Mom's grave with a mix of trepidation and excitement – to find out what sort of vision touching her tombstone might bring. With how low I'm now feeling, maybe it's not such a good idea, but then again, I have to put together the pieces of the puzzle.

"You may as well drive," Dad says, handing me the keys to his truck.

I open the driver's side door and climb in. The seat's freezing, as is the steering wheel. I turn the key, and the engine sluggishly whirs to life with a roar.

When I stop at the top of the driveway, I can spy a slither of blue sky on the horizon and the sun peering over the mountains through the heavy snow. I think back to the start of the year, when the conditions were not that different to now, before carefully pulling out of the driveway.

I drive the whole way into Boulder with neither of us saying a word. I turn into Dad's brickworks and park in front of his office.

"Do you want to go to the ancient Egypt exhibition in Denver with me tomorrow?" I ask. It's been heavy on my mind for a week, and after what William said about reaching out to Dad, I figured what the hell.

He glances over. "I've got stuff that needs doing around the house."

I try hard not to react. I've become used to hearing his excuses.

Without another word, he steps out of the car, and I pull out of the brickworks, backtracking toward the cemetery. *Oh well, at least I tried!*

I quickly turn my thoughts to more pressing matters.

The last vision I had, of Ammit chasing me, after touching Mom's tombstone is still so fresh in my mind. I wonder if by touching her tombstone, I'm actually seeing into the Duat. I wonder if I can control it.

What does it have to do with the other visions, where I'm journeying through the Duat on the Mesektet, though? Last night, where Anubis turned into a shadowy mass was terrifying.

When I pull into the cemetery, there isn't a soul to be seen. It's still snowing fairly heavily, and it's done a decent job of hiding all the tombstones. I kill the engine and listen to the wind howl through the gaps in the truck's doors and windows.

As I approach Mom's tombstone, I look around one last time to make sure I'm alone, then kneel before it.

"Hi Mom," I say, choking on my words.

I can't believe how much this still hurts. My heart aches as I picture her face.

"I wish I was with you," I whisper.

I reach out with a shaky hand. This time I try to control the vision, to try and make sense of the loss. As expected, a vision instantly comes to me ...

> *I'm surrounded by dark hallways of limestone. The air is warm, and a foul stench carries on the breeze. This is just like last time. I hear heavy footsteps and know to whom they belong: Ammit, Swallower of the Dead, is ahead.*

I pull my hand away, my heart racing and my breathing heavy. My breath mists the icy air. *Damn.* Why would I see the same thing? I draw a deep, stuttered breath and try to calm my nerves. Before reaching out again, I try to place myself at the western akhet in my mind's eye ...

I stand before an inverted pyramidal portal made of onyx and gold; it's Anubis' portal. I stare at the black inky surface as a reflection slowly develops. I'm in my normal form, as I appear on Earth. Running my hands over my face, my heart races. My normal human face stares back as I'm gripped with curiosity.

Something whisks past me like a gust, and I spin around in fright. A black amorphous cloud, a shadowy mass with ribbon-like tentacles for wings, is flying around me, circling me. It looks just like the shadowy mass that Anubis turned into in my last vision. It's him, it has to be. I become dizzy with every turn. My heart hammers in my chest.

I pull my hand away from Mom's tombstone, gasping for breath, my mind jumbled in confusion and feeling dizzy. *What the hell was that?*

I had hoped being able to control the visions into the Duat would answer some questions, but it has only left me with more. Why would I appear in the Duat as I do on Earth? Why was Anubis – if that shadowy mass was indeed him – circling me? Was he about to attack? It doesn't add up.

In all my other visions, I am Anubis.

I can't believe I can actually control the visions – to some degree. I shake my head, trying to clear my mind as I stand. I can't take much more of this insanity. Once the adrenaline wears off, the biting cold begins to hit me. With a heavy face, I turn and head back to the truck.

On the way home from the cemetery, I pull up out the front of Belinda's house. It's stopped snowing, but the ground is covered in four or five inches of snow. I walk up the front steps, tapping my toes against the timber steps as I go to knock off the snow. Belinda's mom reversing out of their garage, on her way to work, catches my eye. We smile and wave to one another.

Belinda answers the door; her hair is still messy from having recently woken.

Behind her, Warren is sitting in his armchair, reading the paper and holding a cup of coffee. I can see the steam rising from it against the cold air.

"There's a fresh brew in the kitchen if you want one," he says.

Belinda points toward the kitchen with her head before turning, and I follow. I sit on a stool at the kitchen bench. "Did you get the potassium nitrate from the agricultural cooperative?" I say quietly, looking back toward the living room to make sure Warren's out of earshot.

She hands me a coffee with a grin. "Yeah, no sweat."

"Five pounds?" I ask.

"Yeah. The guy didn't even ask what it was for."

I smile. I thought asking for a lot would make it sound like it's for fertilizer rather than anything untoward.

She chuckles and continues, "Who in their right mind would want to make fifteen pounds of black powder?"

We laugh and sit together drinking our coffees. I don't know at what point I could call Belinda my girlfriend, but I suspect we'd have to go on at least one date first. Thinking about the exhibition, I try to think of a way to ask her if she'd like to go, without it sounding like a date.

"There's an exhibition on at the Denver Museum about ancient Egypt … would you like to go to it tomorrow?"

I'm glad I extended an olive branch to Dad, but I'm even more glad that he said no. I'd much rather go with Belinda.

She smiles. "Yeah, that'd be nice."

I feel a warmth in my heart, a noticeable break from the pain of depression.

We finish our coffees and head into her room. She pulls out a large brown paper bag from her wardrobe and hands it to me. It is filled with white powder – potassium nitrate. *Damn, five pounds is a lot.*

I close the bag and hand it back to her. She puts it back in her wardrobe and sits down next to me on the bed.

"I visited Mom's grave this morning," I say.

"It would have been nice if we could have gone to the exhibition with your mom."

I give her a half-smile. I'm so lucky to have her as a friend. Without her, my life would be permanently dark, pointless. "I miss her so much."

Belinda doesn't say anything, but I can see a sadness in her eyes.

"I sometimes wish I died in the accident," I blurt out.

She gasps and grabs my hand, clenching it. "Why?" she asks softly.

"I don't know ... so I could be with Mom ... to get away from Dad. Since the accident, I've not even been afraid of death." I empty my lungs and Belinda holds my hand even tighter. "I just don't see the point in going on." Even as I'm saying the words, I know it's a mistake, but I can't stop myself. I'm such an idiot. She's probably going to run a mile now.

Belinda shakes her head. "I can't imagine what you've gone through. But you won't always feel this way. You never know ... maybe in time, you and your dad will become close."

"I doubt it," I say, trying to pull myself together. "I've given up on him. I can't be bothered."

She looks down at our hands. Under any normal circumstance, I'd be ecstatic, her holding my hand. It is after all our first real physical contact.

I have to find an escape from feeling so horrid, time to embrace my darker side, time to flirt with death. All I can seem to focus on is the idea of making the black powder.

"Do want to go into town … to the Ag co-op to buy the sulfur?"

Belinda nods. "I'll just get changed."

I try to read her face, unsure if I should stay or go.

Belinda laughs with raises eyebrows. "Get out!"

A grin breaks through my heavy face. *Okay, now I know.* As I get up, she punches me hard on the shoulder. My grin sets.

I have butterflies in my stomach as we pull up out the front of the Ag co-op. There's a drive-through for loading trucks with supplies that we could have pulled into, but I guess with Belinda in the car we better not. If the same guy's working, he might remember her and think it's dubious that we're back for more chemicals.

"Should I get out, so you can drive through?" Belinda asks, almost as if reading my mind.

"I guess … it might seem more feasible … like I have nothing to hide if I drive through."

Belinda jumps out. "I'll meet you around the back."

As she walks off, I pull into the drive-through. There are stacks of hay bales and live-stock feed in white hessian sacks on the one side. Cobwebs cover timber rafters, agricultural implements are scattered all over the place, and several pallets of dog food are stacked near the counter. An old man approaches, and I jump out to greet him, my heart racing. We could get into serious trouble if they piece together that we intend to make black powder.

"Good morning, son. What can I do for you?" the man croaks.

"Dad asked me to get him some fertilizer ... sulfur, I think he said," I lie, but it's not like I'm about to tell him the truth.

The man doesn't even bat an eyelid. "Sure, son. Follow me."

I follow him into a room toward the end of the drive-through. He has a bad hunch and favors his left leg. He's wearing corduroy pants and a flannel shirt. Considering how cold it is, he must be made of tough stuff.

"Aren't you cold?" I say, trying to make small talk, to take his mind off any suspicious thoughts he may have about me.

He gives me a wicked smile, showing that several teeth are missing. "Not likely. How much does he want?" he asks as he cracks the lid of a plastic barrel.

"Ah ... five pounds ... I think."

He scoops the sulfur into a brown paper bag and weighs it on some old scales that hang from the rafters. It reminds me of the weighing of the heart ceremony in the Duat – a soul's eventual judgement. Although I don't recall there being anything in the forty-two negative confessions like '*Thou shall not make explosives.*'

"Anything else, son?" he asks, handing me the bag.

"That's it. Thank you."

After paying, I jump back into the truck. When I pull out of the drive-through, I spot Belinda a short distance down the road and pull over.

"Who did you get?" she asks as she climbs in.

"Not the same guy ... this one was really old."

Belinda smiles.

The following morning, we arrive at the Denver Museum. I've been ardent about coming to see the ancient Egypt exhibition ever since William told me about it. Belinda's wearing a floral shirt and a cream jacket that looks really warm – a break from her usual tomboy style. I notice she's not even wearing her usual nail earrings. A long yawn escapes me as I kill the engine. A little embarrassed, I give Belinda a smile. I'm excited about going out with her, but I still can't shake the darkness of sorrow and despair. I regret telling her as much as I did.

"What's wrong?" she asks, her cheerful glow fading.

Feeling even worse now that my mood is rubbing off on her, I just shake my head.

"What's wrong?" she insists as we head toward the entrance.

"I'm just tired ... I didn't get any sleep last night."

"You need coffeeee!" she says in a whimsical voice, her round eyes sparkling.

We both laugh. We walk toward the exhibition, where a lady greets us and tears off our ticket stubs. The entrance is a black, dimly lit hallway. It feels as though we're stepping into the Underworld. As we step into the darkness, Belinda reaches out and holds my hand. I'm trying really hard to not look over and just act all nonchalant, but my curiosity gets the better of me. She gives me a tiny smile.

In the next room, there are three limestone reliefs behind glass. The carvings show people and hieroglyphs and have museum labels below.

Belinda stops and reads one of the labels. "What's BCE?"

"Before Common Era, it's a culturally neutral term. It's the same as BC."

She takes a look at the tablet and gasps. "That's four thousand years old!"

I nod. It's one thing I love about the Egyptian culture. Now here, all I can think about is Mom and how much I miss her. I'm starting to understand why Dad didn't want to come here with me. I can imagine even he would get teary-eyed with so many reminders of our time in Egypt. Was coming here with Belinda such a good idea? I hope I can keep it together. I have to; I can't lose her too.

As we continue on, my depression only gets worse.

We look at four Canopic jars behind glass, and I try to blink away my tears. Belinda glances at me. I suspect she can tell something's wrong, but all she does is grip my hand a little tighter.

"Qebehsenuef, Hapy, Duamutef, and Imsety," she says, stumbling on their names.

"They're the Four Sons of Horus," I say.

The next room is filled with mummies, timber coffins, jewelry, and a timber funerary bark. A million memories come flooding back.

Belinda leads me over to the mummy. The bandages are a really dark brown and purposefully wound around its small body. Beside it is an eloquently painted coffin. Although it's thousands of years old, it's still in excellent condition. I can't imagine the time it would take to make a coffin like that. I picture Mom's coffin as it was lowered into the ground. Now, a couple of months later, I can imagine her going-forth-by-day. Maybe she'll visit me in an incorporeal sense once she reaches the Field of Reeds – the desired outcome in the afterlife once passing your judgement.

I feel my face tighten. This was a bad idea coming here with Belinda. I stare at the mummy, torn between fascination and wanting to leave. My heart's racing as my emotions jumble. I can feel Belinda staring at me.

"Are you thinking about your mom?" she asks softly.

I nod, sick of feeling like this. Remembering her funeral is making me wonder when mine will be. If I keep messing around with copper bombs and black powder, maybe it will be soon …

She grabs my hand and leads me over to the next display. "What's a bark?" she asks, trying to lighten the mood. She knows how much I love talking about all things Egyptian.

"It's a generic term for a boat," I say, taking the bait. "They believed that the Sun God, Ra, journeyed through the sky on his day-bark and died of an evening, at which point he became Atum. He entered the Duat in the west and traveled to the east on his night-bark and was then reborn the following day as Khepri."

"What? He becomes a different god?"

"No, all the same god, the chief celestial deity, they're just different monikers."

"What does 'Khepri' mean?" she asks. She always sounds so fascinated. I love that her interest is genuine.

"Khepri is the morning sun. The ancient Egyptians had strong concepts of symbolism and duality. They used the scarab beetle, or dung beetle, to depict Khepri, because it pushes a ball of dung across the desert, which could be thought of like the journey of the sun through the sky. The scarab beetle lay lava in the ball of dung and when they mature, they burst out of the ball fully formed. So, the scarab's ball was also a symbol of rebirth."

"Oh, I get it. So, Ra dies of an evening and was reborn every morning, and the scarab symbolizes that rebirth."

"Yeah, that's it."

"What's duality?"

"It's when something has two components or two meanings, such as chaos and order, life and death, or light and dark. Sekhmet and Hathor are a good example: Hathor was a creator or mother deity, and Sekhmet was a destroyer. They were considered two aspects of the one deity, the Eye of Ra.

"Or the waters of Nun that Ra's bark journeyed on through the Duat. If you fell into the waters of Nun, you would cease to exist, to die a second death, but the waters of Nun also had a regenerative aspect because they carried Ra through the Duat to rebirth. The duality of the waters of Nun reflect the duality of the river Nile, the lifeblood of Egypt, in that the Nile could bring new life through silt and nutrient deposits when it flooded, but could also bring death by drowning, or even crocodile and hippopotamus attacks."

"Oh, wow. I can't believe how deep their concepts are. I can see why you love it. You know, you become a different person when you talk about this stuff, all energetic and animated."

I return her smile. I love the mythology, but it's the deep concepts of the soul and the afterlife that truly speak to me. It's a connection I shared with Mom that we will have for eternity – one that will hopefully bring us together again someday.

We move on and stand before a great statue of Anubis. It is nearly completely black and towers above us. With the head of a jackal, he is wearing a kilt and is standing with one arm outstretched holding a was scepter. In the other hand, he's holding an ankh – the symbol of immortality and life. He looks like he's standing guard, watching over the dead.

I stare at Anubis, recalling my vivid visions. I can't take my eyes off him. He has such a mystical quality about him. Reading *The Egyptian Book of the Dead* has helped me understand the passage through the Duat, but it has done little to explain my visions. Why would I appear as Anubis in my visions? Part of me wonders whether in a past life I was Anubis, in all his majesty.

Belinda rocks our hands from side to side to get my attention, and realize I was probably staring at Anubis, caught up in my mind.

As we leave the exhibition, we step out of the darkness and into the light. I can't help but think that that's a suitable metaphor to apply to my life: how I need to wallow less in the darkness, thinking of what I've lost, and start thinking about today and what I have.

But then again, there's comfort in the darkness.

Sitting in the museum's cafeteria, we eat our lunch. Belinda is smiling to herself. It's a faint smile, but noticeable. As I drink my coffee, I study her face.

She notices me looking and her eyebrows edge down. "What?"

I shake my head.

She pauses awhile. I can see the gears turning in her head. "Was this a date?" she finally asks.

My heart skips a beat. I was hoping this question could fly under the radar and for this to be an informal date. "Ah ... I don't know ... I guess so."

She blushes and looks down at her coffee cup.

As we head back to the carpark, I reach out to hold her hand. Belinda is looking radiant. A sense of happiness warms my heart, it's like the sun bursting through an overcast sky. This feeling is so similar to when I'm holding Anput's hand in the Duat. It's so intense, I'm starting to believe that Belinda is my soulmate.

When I have to leave her, I start to feel blue, not wanting to say goodbye.

"Did you want to help me fit the pistons this afternoon?" I ask. I wasn't going to work on my car, but I ask so I can spend more time with her.

"Yeah, sure." She stops walking, pulls me in close and gives me a kiss on the lips.

My heart is racing and I'm grinning as I'm overcome with euphoria.

"I was going to do that at the cafeteria, but I chickened out," she says.

Belinda's such a great friend, and I guess, now my "girlfriend." However, I still can't understand why I don't feel good all the time we are together. It seems that there are still times when my depression comes back when I'm seemingly happy, and it comes back with a vengeance.

After a long afternoon of working on the engine, Belinda and I have the pistons in and heads on, and we are about to down tools when I hear a car coming down the driveway.

"That's Dad," Belinda says, clearly recognizing the sound of his truck well before I picked it out.

Warren climbs out, looks Belinda in the eye, and points toward his truck with his head to call her over. I can see where Belinda gets the head point thing from. I walk over, smiling inwardly. I feel so much better being around Belinda and her dad. I wish I could live with them instead.

Belinda slides a small cardboard box out of her dad's truck and holds it out to me, her arms straining a little under some mysterious weight.

I puzzle. "What's this?"

Warren grabs the cloth covering something inside and pulls it away, revealing a carburetor. It's big, looks like it would fit a vee-eight and has Holley written on the side.

"It's for your Mustang," he says with a joyous smile.

I look at him dumbfounded and shake my head to clear my confusion. "What ... for me to buy?"

"No ... it's a gift! I couldn't do any heavy lifting, but I scrounged together some parts and rebuilt it. It's a Holley four-barrel six-fifty."

I'm not sure what that means, but it looks awesome. Belinda is beaming. I guess she knew about this. "I don't know what to say. It must have still cost you ... for a rebuild kit and parts."

Warren shakes his head. "Don't worry about it ... it's my pleasure ... it gave me something to do."

I reach out and take the box, swallowing hard, taken aback that he would do something so nice. "Thank you," I say, getting choked up. "I don't know how to repay you."

"You can take us for a ride once you finish it," Warren says.

The carburetor is such a nice gift – and expensive too. I guess he must like me, but I still can't imagine him wanting Belinda to spend a lot of time with a boy.

I carry the box inside and place it on the bench. "Is your dad okay with you spending all this time with me?" I ask Belinda, before Warren can catch up and hear me.

"Yeah. He likes you."

I give her a tiny smile, pinching my eyebrows together. I don't know why he likes me; I don't even like me most of the time.

Chapter 12

The darkest hour of the night is also the greatest. Air thick
with tension, Shani sits alongside Anput before the timber
plinth upon which Atum lies. Isis and Nephthys stand by
his side.

"O Lord Anubis," Shani says as she stands. "What
purpose would Aya's and Eman's hearts have to the
thief?"

I look down into Shani's eyes. "The reason for the
theft, I am unsure. Though terrifying the consequences if
left unchecked, for in the Duat, the fate of all existence
can be decided."

"When we reach the Hall of the Two Truths, if the
gods of the council look into my heart, will they see my
guilt?" Shani asks. "Will they see the same guilt when they
look into the heart of Tau?"

"The Osiris Shani, your soul is so much more than
your worst, or best act; it is the sum of your time on
Earth. It is that sum that will be weighed against the

feather of Maat. You cannot compare yourself to Tau, for he led a life of corruption."

Shani forces a smile.

I am afraid for her, for although I see her for the pure soul that she is, she still must release her burden of guilt before we reach the Hall of the Two Truths.

I leave Shani and go to my birth mother. "O Nephthys, what do you know of Tau?"

"He was well known on Earth as a thief," Nephthys says. "He showed nay remorse for his actions and will not last the night, I am certain of it."

"When he was on Earth, did he work alone, or did he have an accomplice?"

"He always worked alone," Nephthys says.

Isis joins us. Standing together, the sisters look so much alike.

"O Isis, what purpose would Aya's and Eman's hearts have for the thief?" I ask the same question that Shani did unto me. "You mentioned for all manner of creatures. Do you think whomever stole them desires to create a creature to disrupt the balance of power in the Duat?"

"Anubis, I do not think so, for Aya and Eman lived wholesome lives and are simple farmers. To create a wicked creature, the thief would need a wicked heart, plus they would need to know the words to speak to breathe life into that clay form," Isis says.

"Then for what purpose? I do not understand."

Nephthys' and Isis' faces are somber as we contemplate the situation.

"I am afraid," I say, "for we approach midnight and the answers to these terrible questions still elude us. I fear for whatever purpose the hearts and the clay have, that we will be too late, and all could be lost on this night – in this realm and in the mundane world. I am torn, for my foremost duty is to prepare the Osiris Shani for her judgement and help protect the Mesektet, but I must also search for the thief."

"Anubis. Not alone are thou. For together we will find the languid one who would steal. Do not fear, for your father, Osiris, Foremost of the Westerners, will not allow this corruption to go unchecked," Isis says, but I see that her attention is drawn to something else.

I follow the direction of her gaze and see Shani standing, staring over the prow, frozen like her shabti.

I go to her side. "What is it, the Osiris Shani?"

"O Lord Anubis, there is something heading our way. I cannot see it but I … can feel it."

My heart lights with warmth, for I know that of what she speaks. "Do not be afraid. It is the Great Scarab."

Shani draws a deep breath and studies my face. Ahead, flying over the flowing waters of Nun, the Great Scarab flutters with a sole destination in mind. As the Mesektet journeys forward, the Scarab flies over our heads. Its colorful emerald wings sparkle in the dim light as they beat back and forth.

We group around the timber plinth with honor and reverence – for only a few have ever witnessed the majesty of Atum being reborn as Khepri.

The Great Scarab hovers atop Atum's chest.

Shani clenches my hand. Isis and Nephthys bow, their hands clasped to their chests.

The Great Scarab magically descends through Atum's bandages, through his chest and directly into his heart. The two incorporeal beings blend in an extraordinary display like two clouds becoming one.

Upon their joining, Atum's heart glows orange, pulsing brighter and brighter. The ram head of Atum slowly changes shape, becoming less pointed and more round, gradually changing into that of a scarab beetle. His new scarab head is nearly as large as his torso. The Great God lies on the timber plinth, motionless. Not fully reborn is he, but he is now Khepri. His heart glows but his fate is not secured, for Khepri must face his demon, in this, the darkest hour of the night.

"O Lord Anubis, is Khepri rejuvenated now?" Shani asks.

"Not fully, that will take until the time of dawn. He has power but still relies on his entourage for protection."

Shani looks up, and with a glowing face says, "Atum becometh Khepri, Khepri becometh Ra, Ra becometh Atum."

I smile with joy. "The circle of life. So has it been for millions of years, and so will it be for millions more."

Shani reveres in the orange glow. I place my hand on her shoulder and then lead her toward the prow. The Mesektet gathers speed, and Isis leaves Khepri's side to join us. I look into my mother's eyes and her eyes look into mine, for we know why the waters of Nun make haste. The sandy shore is baron, not a ba to be seen. Faster and faster the bark speeds. Shani wears her fear upon her face.

Thoth steps down from the prow and joins us, with Isis taking his place.

"O Lord Thoth, what is happening?" Shani asks.

"Isis, Goddess of Magic and Spells, is about to use her most powerful akhu. Spells that only she knows, for they are the greatest of all."

"Why does only she know them?"

"Her most powerful akhu, if recited wrong, could destroy the subterranean sphere, the celestial sphere, and the mundane world. Her most powerful akhu is not even recorded in my book for fear of falling into the wrong hands."

Shani frowns, clearly unsure what's about to happen, but then she opens her mouth wide when she sees what lies a short distance ahead.

Apophis, Lord of Chaos, is in our path, his gray serpent body so wide it spreads between the sandy banks of the great river. Even his hissing split tongue is longer than the bark. With his jaws open, he's devouring the flowing waters of Nun, his throat so large it could swallow the Mesektet whole. Large poisonous fangs hang from his upper jaw, ready to strike.

The water crashes and rumbles as it builds speed, threatening to wreck the bark.

Isis stands in the prow, her hands raised to the sky, and as she speaks her spell, black and gray storm clouds gather, swirling and hardening. Storm clouds light up as lightning flashes. The Mesektet rushes forward at a frightful rate.

Shani clasps my hand as we hold on for dear life.

Two streams of lightning fly out of the clouds, connecting with Isis' palms in a continuous crackling of white light. Isis holds the lightning for a second, pushes, and the lightning flows back up into the clouds. The storm clouds light up. Six massive lightning bolts explode out of the clouds, striking Apophis' long serpentine back. It strikes over and over in a blinding display of raw power.

Apophis' gray scales turn charcoal black as though he's been torched by extreme fire, and the lightning stops. As we bare down on Apophis, cracks start appearing in his charcoaled body. Just as we reach the threshold of the serpent's jaws, his body explodes in a cloud of ash that flies into the sky. One of his fangs – only half-turned unto ash – plummets from above. We all watch opened mouthed as it strikes Khepri's chest like a dagger.

It drives deep into his heart, only stopping when it hits the timber plinth beneath with a thud. The vast majority is still protruding with only the roundest part turned unto ash.

We have to save him. If Khepri doesn't survive, if he is not reborn, the mundane world will also die. Shani screams in terror. We rush to Khepri's side as the raging waters ease and the cloud of ash falls upon the land. I stand on one side of the timber plinth while Anput stands on the other. My heart thunders. We reach out and grasp the fang and pull. When it comes out, the whole fang slowly turns unto ash. Flecks on the surface glow red-hot before breaking away and floating off.

"Why did the fang survive Isis' akhu?" Shani asks.

"Apophis is cunning," I say. "He receded into the fang therewith murderous intent, and the powers of the Great Scarab is rejuvenating the ba of Apophis."

More and more of the fang breaks away, and then in a cascade of red-hot fiery embers, the whole thing breaks up and rises into the air.

We watch as Khepri's heart then glows orange, the Great Scarab trying hard to heal his heart and mind.

"Isis, should we call upon Selket, Protectress of the Dead?"

Isis bows toward me. "My words have journeyed on Shu, and Selket has heard them. Sleep fell from the eyelids of the scorpion goddess and she awoke. In her presence we soon shall be."

Knowing the scorpion goddess will be with us soon brings me great comfort.

The waters of Nun settle and resume their steady march east. Thoth takes up his position again in the prow, and Isis and Nephthys resume theirs, standing guard by Khepri's side.

A silence has fallen over the land and there is little to behold in the darkest hour of the night.

I fear for Khepri as we wait, for these are the realms of Sokar, Apophis, and Seth, where all is inimical, where all could be lost. We all share that fear, worn on our faces. Selket appears to the east, the deathstalker scorpion's giant yellow-green body and legs towering above the bark as she nears. Horus steers toward an alcove to meet her at the shore.

"O Selket," Nephthys says when we are close enough. "The Great God has been stung by Apophis. Will thou seize the poison within his ba?"

Selket nears the waters and raises her giant tail high. "The bane of Apophis I will absorb."

Her long yellow-green tail uncoils over the water and settles, poised above Khepri's chest. Drops of venom rise from the Great God's chest, drip upward and are absorbed by Selket's stinger. Drop after drop rises, and soon the venom is magically drawn from Khepri's chest.

When there is nay more, Selket withdraws her tail and steps back from the shore. "It is done, O Nephthys."

Khepri's chest pulses orange again, steadily growing stronger. His whole body begins to glow, and then – leaving his mummiform body upon the timber plinth – a second form of the Great God rises. As he rises, he sits upright and unfolds his wings from his scarab beetle head.

The skin of the second form of Khepri burns with intense heat and light like the surface of the sun. Using his flaming wings, he flies into the air and lands upon the shore. The flaming form grows, doubling in size and then doubling once more. His skin is of flame and harsh to the eyes. The sky is filled with light as Khepri gets down on one knee, his huge form towering above the bark.

Khepri speaks in a booming voice. "My entourage, you serve me well in my hour of need. Wait for Selket and I, for Apophis must be restrained."

We all bow in reverence.

A swishing sound, like sand sliding across the desert, carries through the air. It's hard to tell what direction it's coming from, but I know that of which it belongs to. Over the stern of the Mesektet, a gray slithering creature draws near. It is Apophis, his head kept low and jaws clenched.

He surges forward, his split tongue hissing and fangs still dripping with venom.

"Anubis," Shani sputters in fright as the giant serpent closes in faster and faster. "How is he still alive?"

"The ba of Apophis cannot be so easily destroyed. When the fang disintegrated, his ba traveled upon the air, and in nay time at all, it has restored. For the Great Scarab doesn't just bring life unto Atum, but it breathes life unto all."

Khepri steps away from the shore and whips his right fist through the air, drawing out a long rope made of fire, causing thunder to roll across the sky. The fiery rope lies on the sandy desert ground, flaming and sparking hot embers.

Apophis hisses and lunges at Selket, taking her in his mouth, but she's too large to swallow whole. With her tail still protruding from his mouth, she stings him between the eyes. Apophis spits her out, shaking his head violently in shock.

While Apophis is dazed from the sting, and Selket recovers, Khepri rips his fiery rope through the air and lassos one of Apophis' fangs. The rope wraps around the fang several times in a tight bind that crackles with fiery embers. Apophis rears up, pulling Khepri's flaming body into the air in a chaotic struggle. Khepri releases his fiery rope, and using his scarab beetle wings, he lands on the ground.

Apophis raises his head high and coils his body, ready to strike again; his forked tongue lashes the air in a hiss. He strikes, slashing at Khepri with his fangs. Selket raises her tail, her stinger dripping with venom, and drives it into his scaly body. Khepri whips his fiery rope, lassoing the serpent's neck while he's stunned by Selket's venom.

The great serpent thrashes, coils and strikes, unable to get free. Khepri makes a fist with his left hand and whips it through the air, drawing a second fiery rope that lets out another thunderous blast. He lassoes it around Apophis' neck, and now, with two fiery ropes around the giant serpent's neck, he leaps upon his back, pulling him around in circles.

Selket strikes again, and Apophis is finally subdued, slumbering under Selket's venom. Khepri binds the giant serpent securely with the fiery ropes.

Selket and Khepri walk to the shore.

Khepri gets down on one knee, exhausted. "Apophis can try in vain to get free. He will not attack again of this night, for naught can my binds escape."

Isis bows. "Hail unto ye, O Khepri, we will guard ye with our bas. Rest now and be with the Great Scarab."

Khepri rises into the air and flies over the water and above the Mesektet, shrinking down to normal size as he does so. He hovers above his mummiform body, which is lying upon the timber plinth, and as his flaming body descends, it merges into Khepri's mummiform body. His whole being glows orange before slowly dimming.

The sky darkens and silence falls over the land once more.

Nephthys bows. "O Selket, we thank you for your venom. A friend unto the dead indeed you are."

As we leave the shore, I watch Horus working the steering oar as we continue on – though his time is upon him, for Seth lies in wait. Seth is not only Horus' enemy, but my father Osiris' too, and must be defeated at all cost.

Chapter 13

"Kyle," the voice floats through the back of my mind but it doesn't quite register. "Kyle!" The voice becomes clearer, louder, snapping me out of my trance.

I'm in metalwork class, and Mr. Jones is standing before me, his eyebrows pinched together as he stares at me. "Where were you just now? I kept calling you," he says.

I take a deep breath. "Sorry, sir."

"Stop sitting around, get to work!" he says bad-temperedly.

"Yes, sir," I reply.

Damn. Another vision in broad daylight. I look around the room to see if anyone saw me off in a daze, but nobody seems to have noticed.

To hell with doing my metalwork project. I'm so sick of this mundane world. Time to put our black powder plan to work. Belinda's been wanting to build a cannon for some time, and I like the idea of making something dangerous. So, while Mr. Jones is distracted, I get to it.

I cut the three-inch mild steel bar stock to length, roughly ten inches, and place it in the chuck of the lathe, all the while looking over my shoulder. Mr. Jones is busy with another student, so I make the most of it. I quickly machine one end of the round bar and put a small chamfer on it, quickly turn it, repeat, and drill it with a center drill. Once the half-inch drill's in the tailstock, I start drilling.

Craig approaches. "What are you doing?"

"Making a cannon!" I say excitedly.

"What? You're nuts. Mr. Jones will kill you if he catches you."

"If he comes over, distract him," I reply, my heart pounding with adrenaline from the thrill of potentially getting caught.

"Why bother? No one's ever going to sell you gunpowder."

I'm not sure I trust him, so I don't tell him anything more.

Once the bar stock's drilled, I remove it from the lathe and stuff it in my backpack. It clunks against the desk. Logan and Joseph, who are sitting several seats up, both look over.

"What was that?" Logan asks, his face taking on that hard-ass look he usually has, but Joseph has a tiny smile, as if he's just curious about what I'm up to.

"My metalwork project," I reply with a straight face.

"What is it?" Logan blusters.

"None of your business, *dumb-ass!*" I put a lot of emphasis on the final word. I couldn't care less if he hit me again.

Logan gets up from his chair, looking like he's about to start world war three. "What did you call me?"

My heart begins to race. A second passes, and he backs down. It's funny how my not retaliating last time has made him hesitant. Joseph is smirking behind Logan's back, and I turn away.

Mr. Jones is still busy, so I continue with my plan. I pull out some half-inch bar stock and start cutting it up into two-inch lengths. Once I have a dozen, I head back over to the lathe and start machining pointy ends. I look up at the clock at the front of the classroom and realize I don't have much time left if I want to finish all of these cannonballs. I quicken my pace. Joseph and I lock eyes.

He smirks. I guess he can tell I'm not working on my project.

When I'm finished, I shove the bullet-like cannonballs into my backpack, just in time for the bell, which signals the end of the school day.

As I walk toward the front gates, Belinda is standing around with her friends chatting. When she sees me, she makes her way over.

"Hey," I say as I open my backpack for her to peak in. It has some serious weight to it now.

Her face lights up with excitement, and we head toward her dad's truck. It's been snowing hard for this time of year, and there are snowdrifts covering the sides of the footpaths. A passing car slushes through the snow, a sound that still takes my mind back to the accident — and with it come the feelings of despair and heartache.

As we reach Warren's truck, Logan calls out from his imported car, with Joseph by his side, "So, when's your rust bucket going to be finished?"

Belinda winds down her window. "His Mustang will beat your piece of crap!"

Joseph laughs loudly at this, which seems to infuriate Logan even more. Belinda turns to me and we share a smile.

The truck rumbles to life, and as Belinda's about to pull out, Logan tears out of his parking spot, sliding all over the place and cuts her off.

Belinda scowls. "Aaarh ... he's such an idiot."

The world's filled with dickheads like him. And I doubt that's going to change any time soon. I can just imagine Logan landing in a position of authority, bought by his parent's money. Talk about moral degradation. I'd bet anything his kids will turn out just like him, or worse. *We're all screwed.*

The following morning, I walk down to Belinda's with the cannon in my backpack. Warren greets me at the front door and then shuffles over to the dining table where a cup of coffee is steaming. "How's your car going?"

"Good. I was going to fit the timing chain tomorrow and was wondering if you would mind helping? I imagine that's not something you'd want to get wrong."

"Not a problem, I'd love to. You're right ... get that wrong and you'll bend all your valve stems, or worse."

Belinda walks out, and when she sees me, her face lights up. I still can't believe she's my girlfriend; she's so beautiful and so full of life, I can't get enough of her. I know I've contemplated it before, but I'm quite sure now that she is my soulmate.

"We'll be in the shed, Dad," she says.

"Okay, be safe, sweetie."

I follow Belinda to the back door. When we step outside, I ask, "Does your dad mind us using his gear?"

"Na. He doesn't care."

"You didn't tell him what we were doing, did you?"

Belinda glances back over her shoulder at me as she opens the door to the shed. "Yeah. Why?"

I look at her in shock. "What? You're joking, right?"

"No. He doesn't care, as long as we're sensible."

I laugh. "Well, I guess that depends on your definition of 'sensible'." I drop my backpack on the bench and pull out the cannon and all the bullet-like cannonballs, while Belinda turns on her dad's MIG welder and rummages through piles of steel offcuts.

She picks up a cannonball. "You know that using half-inch bar stock makes the cannon the equivalent to a fifty-caliber rifle?"

I chuckle. "I hadn't thought of it like that. I just made it that size cause of the standard bar stock size."

She arranges some steel plates into a base of sorts that we can mount the cannon to, then puts her hair up in a ponytail, tucking her hair down the back of her shirt. When she puts on the welding helmet and picks up the heavy-duty weld gloves, I laugh. She's such a tomboy. I wonder what her friends would think of her if they could see her right now.

"What?"

I smile again. "Nothing."

She gives me a tiny smirk and jerks her head forward and back so the helmet falls down in front of her face. She doesn't hesitate before she starts welding. As I watch her work, against the background sound of high-voltage electricity crackling and sparks flying around her, I think about how proud her dad must be of her.

When the cannon is welded to a solid steel base, Belinda pulls her helmet off. She has a wide red band imprinted on her forehead. She takes her gloves off and holds her hands over the cannon, pretending it's a warm fire. "Aw … nice and toasty."

We've just finished the cannon when her dad walks in. I swallow hard. Dad would shit bricks if he saw us doing something like this, but Warren doesn't seem to be phased by it at all. I wish Dad was more like him. He's a friend *and* a father. He's someone I could do things with.

Warren hobbles over and inspects our handywork. "That should do it."

I wonder how much Belinda's told him, if he knows about us also making black powder.

He picks up one of the bullet-like cannonballs and studies it. "Do you have gunpowder?"

I glance over at Belinda before returning my stare to Warren. "We made some black powder."

"Well ... let's let her rip!" he eventually says with the hint of a child-like grin coming to his face.

Belinda and I laugh.

"We thought we'd take it down to the lake," I say.

Warren purses his lips as he thinks. "Just put it in the dam, there's stuff all water in it. You can fire it at the dam wall on the far side."

"You're not worried about the noise?" I ask.

"Na. If anyone asks, I'll tell 'em I was plinking vermin with my three-o-three."

Belinda grabs the now giant lump of steel and reefs it up to her chest. "You heard the man," she says as she struggles with the weight of the steel. "Grab your gear and the matches."

I follow her, occasionally looking over my shoulder as Warren struggles through the snow, following us along the rough terrain of the paddock. When the dam comes into view, I can see why Warren would suggest it. It's roughly a hundred feet in diameter, with high walls and hardly any water.

Belinda uses her foot to scrape away a patch of snow on the ground before dropping the cannon down. I get the black powder from the backpack and am about to pour it down the barrel when Warren finally catches up.

"How much powder do you plan on using?" he asks.

"I was going to use a film canister," I say, trying to read his face.

"Why don't you just start with half a canister?" he counters.

I think about it for a second. *That's not a bad idea actually, considering we've never fired it before.* "Yeah, okay. Sounds good."

After loading the cannon, I roll some black powder in some tissue paper and insert it into the cannon as a wick. I double check it's pointed at the opposite wall of the dam. Belinda moves to stand next to her dad, who is off to the side and ten feet back. After lighting the wick with a match, I run to join her.

The wick burns down. We wait with bated breath.

The thud is really deep and solid, and the cannon rears up as smoke pours from its barrel. A cloud of dirt explodes out of the snow and into the air on the far wall of the dam.

That was intense.

Belinda laughs animatedly.

"Talk about starting your spring break with a bang," Warren says, smiling as he turns and hobbles back to the house.

I watch him walk for some time. The smile on his face doesn't wane.

"You're mad!" Belinda says. "Let's do it again."

I laugh – her enthusiasm is infectious.

It's the following day, and Warren and Belinda have just helped me fit the timing chain when Dad returns from work. That says everything; my own dad's chosen to spend Sunday morning at work, leaving my girlfriend's dad to help me with my car. I should just go and live with Belinda and her family.

Warren reaches out to shake Dad's hand. "Hi, I'm Warren ... Belinda's father."

Dad stops dead in his tracks, almost as if he's seen a ghost, and awkwardly says, "Ah ... Hi, I'm Mark," and then continues into the house.

He's such an ass.

Warren tilts his head to one side, frowning.

"Don't take it personally," I say. "He's like that with everyone." It's a bit of an exaggeration, but I don't want Warren to feel bad.

"Well ... we best get going. Let me know if you need a hand with anything else, okay?"

"Will do. Thanks for all your help, it's really appreciated," I reply.

"Don't mention it, buddy."

After saying goodbye to Warren and Belinda, I head inside. Anger rises from the pit of my stomach like a volcano. *Stuff it.* I'm not going to let Dad off easy for being so cold to Warren. I find him inside angrily stuffing the fireplace with more wood.

"Why did you have to be so rude to Warren?" I snap.

He looks up. "I don't want you hanging around with Belinda or her dad ... got it?" His face is already starting to turn red.

"Why? What's wrong with Belinda and Warren? They're good people."

"He's lazy and a welfare leach! You have to work hard if you want to make something of yourself," Dad yells.

My anger erupts. "What do you know?"

Dad stands, shaking his head, and yells, "That's it. You're banned from seeing Belinda ever again. Got it?"

"Do you know why Warren can't work?" I yell. "A car fell on him at work and broke his back. It took him years just to get back on his feet. He doesn't work because he *can't*. He hobbles around his house like he's seventy."

Dad shakes his head. It's as if he's not heard a word I just said. "You're not seeing her anymore, and that's final!"

Screw him.

I storm off to my room, slamming the door so hard my calendar falls off the wall. I pace back and forth, wanting to tear my bedroom to pieces to release my anger.

Just when I feel like I'm getting my life back together it all falls apart. *I hate Dad.* A tear streaks down my cheek as I feel Mom's feather of Maat amulet through my shirt. I wish it was him that died in the accident instead of her.

I think back to the article in the paper about the truck driver killing himself. If he succumbed to depression, while supported by a kind, loving family, what chance do I have? I'm sick of feeling this way. Broken. I'm completely powerless. Maybe I'm destined to feel this way for all of eternity, in this life and the next. I stare at the white landscape outside and picture the darkness of the Duat, the silence, wishing I was there instead. I'm sick of this life. I wish I could just be with Mom again.

The following day, I trudge through the snow to William's office. He's standing at the front door, looking out.

"How about that snow," he says when I reach him.

"It seems to be easing up," I mumble.

William gestures to the hallway with an open palm. We enter the room and I fall onto the couch. I feel talking with William these past few months has been helping, but I haven't been looking forward to today.

"How have you been?"

I shake my head and look away. I blink away my tears as anger and hopelessness flood my mind. "Not good."

"Your medication hasn't been working?"

"No. It's not just that. Dad's banned me from seeing Belinda," I say as I wipe my watery eyes and the soft palate of my throat aches.

I'm surprised to see that William looks upset at this. "I'm sorry to hear that," he says. "Why did he do that?"

I shake my head. "He's an ass, that's why! He keeps calling Belinda's dad a bum, because he doesn't work, but what he didn't know was that Belinda's dad was in an accident and *can't* work."

"Did you tell him that?"

"Yeah," I reply, trying to suppress my anger so it doesn't sound like I'm raising my voice at William.

"That's not good," he says softly.

"Tell me about it. And because I've been spending so much time with Belinda, Craig and I see much less of each other. Now I'm all alone again."

William stares at me, which makes me feel uncomfortable. I try to tell myself he's just taking his time reading my body language.

Finally, he speaks. "This may seem a little off topic, but bear with me. Do you try to show others compassion?"

I nod. I haven't been great at it, but I have been trying harder to show others compassion and respect. It's what Mom would've wanted.

"Do you show your dad that same compassion?"

I think hard for a moment. "Probably not," I finally concede. "I think I give him a harder time."

"It would be good if you could. Your dad's what, forty-two, and he's lost two wives? He's been through a lot, as have you. I'm not excusing him for not being there for you, but sometimes we need to cut each other a break."

I nod again, knowing deep down that William's right.

"Why don't you try talking with your dad? See if you can patch things up?"

The thought of it seems so impossible that I shake my head. "Why's it gotta be so hard?"

"It's hard because you've had a hard life. But it will get easier. It won't always be this hard. Trust me, I know." William looks sad for a moment, as if he's somewhere else entirely, and then just as quickly, he's back in the room and giving me a focused look. "Do you extend that compassion to yourself?"

"What do you mean?" I ask.

"You also need to cut yourself a break from time to time too ... to show yourself some kindness."

I smile inwardly. "I've never even thought of doing that."

"You should," William says, then pauses for a moment. "Have you had any thoughts of self-harm?"

I hesitate, not sure whether I should say anything, but then decide to be honest, I know I can trust William. "I often wish I died in the accident. I sometimes picture jumping off a bridge or shooting myself."

"Do you have a plan?"

"No."

"How have you been sleeping?" William asks.

"Not good. A couple times a week I don't even fall asleep."

"It's been a month now …" William says as he reads through my file. "Do you mind if we try another antidepressant?"

"No." *I'm sick of all this.* "Just when I thought I was getting my life back together again, it all falls apart."

"You've made excellent progress," William says calmly. "You've hit a bump in the road, but all is not lost. You can still say that Belinda and Craig are friends. This might not sound like a consolation, but learning what antidepressants don't work *is* progress. It means we're several steps closer to finding one that does."

I try hard to smile, my despair somewhat easing at this "progress."

"Do you have any good days?"

"I wouldn't say good days, but good moments. They're like cloud breaks in an overcast sky, where for a moment, I feel my depression lift."

"What does that tell you?" he asks, without giving me an opportunity to respond. "That above the clouds is a sky full of sunshine."

The corner of mouth turns up in a crooked smile. "That's a nice sentiment."

"Are you still engaging in risky behavior? Have you made any more copper bombs?"

I give William a thin smile. "We made a cannon the other day. We fired it at Belinda's place."

William raises his eyebrows. "Did you get in trouble at all?"

"Na. Belinda's dad was there."

"You need to be careful," William says, obviously concerned. "It's quite common for people suffering with depression to participate in high-risk activities. Let me ask you something; do you feel like you have a future?"

I shake my head, unable to picture a world in which I have a place.

"It's important to feel you have a future. If you feel you have something to look forward to, then even if you feel really down now, you will have a sense that it won't always hurt this bad. Do you think about what you'd like to do after school?"

I can't picture my life any further than a few weeks from today. I can't picture ever finishing my car. Especially now I'm not allowed to see Belinda. I can't picture finishing school, or Dad and I ever patching things up.

William takes my silence as a no. "Between now and our next session," he says, "I'd like you to put some time aside to think about what you'd like to do after you graduate. Will you do that for me?"

I nod, thinking about how helpful these sessions have been for me. William's wise, and I know I should listen to him more. Maybe he's the one that actually helps me through all this, and I should stop looking for answers in *The Egyptian Book of the Dead* or my visions. One memory from Egypt still haunts me, even when I buried it years ago. It's like that day has a life of its own. Maybe it's time to be completely honest with him – to dig it back up and finally confront it.

"What are you thinking about?" William asks. "You appear deep in thought."

"I ... I have to apologize to you," I say, my heart speeding up at the thought of coming clean.

"Oh ... why's that?" he asks, shifting his weight on where he sits on the couch.

"I lied to you about Ramsi ... when I said the plant in Cairo shut down due to a malfunction."

"Oh?"

I try to bring myself to say the words, but I can't.

I thought I had buried the memory of that day so far in the back of my mind that I'd never recall it again, but as I picture it, I cringe.

"Ramsi and his dad didn't leave," I say, suddenly feeling the need to gasp for air, "Ramsi was killed; he was crushed in the brick press. I saw the whole thing." A tear streaks down my cheek; I don't even bother wiping it away, there's no hiding the torment I feel.

William's mouth pops open; he's clearly trying to hide his surprise, but it's in vain. I guess he's imagining how graphic it must have been, seeing a teenage boy crushed in a gigantic brick press. "I'm sorry to hear that, but you have nothing to apologize for."

For a moment it's like all the oxygen has been sucked out of the room. Neither of us speak.

"Your dad knows you saw that?" he says, looking at me with an intensity I've not seen on him before. I'm not sure whether he's telling me or asking, I guess he's asking.

I shake my head vaguely. "I don't think so."

I thought I was clever burying those memories, but now, two and a half years later, I can't help but wonder if that was when my depression started.

I lost Ramsi in such a horrific way, then Mom, and now I've lost Belinda too. I'm destined to be alone.

After a long and exhausting session with William, I step outside into the chilly afternoon air. It's the first day off school on spring break, and I feel like hell. It's too early to pick Dad up, but there's not enough time to go home either, so I decide to visit Mom's grave.

I buy some flowers and drive out to the cemetery. The last vision I had when touching Mom's tombstone was of being circled by a dark ominous cloud – Anubis, I assume. It was terrifying yet exhilarating too. I've been eagerly awaiting another visit so I could see what else the Duat had in store for me.

I hope Mom doesn't mind me using her tombstone in this way, but then I realize, she'd probably encourage it. I might even only have this power because of her anyway.

When I arrive, I search the area to make sure I'm alone, once again. The coast is clear.

I kneel before her tombstone and place the flowers at its base.

"I wish I was with you, Mom," I say, reaching out and touching the gray granite ...

The air is warm and dry. The desert sands span as far as the eye can see. I'm all alone. Somehow, I will myself to fly, and I soar over the desert like a bird.

I follow a great river eastward until I come across a large limestone building. I don't recall ever seeing it before, but I know in my heart it's the Hall of the Two Truths, where a soul goes to be judged in the afterlife.

Beyond the building is the Field of Reeds — vast waterways upon the shore on which barley grows, and the blessed dead harvest plentiful crops. Timber barks cruise on the calm blue waters between the crops.

I'd like to stay here forever, to dwell with my mother in peace, but my control over this vision is slipping. I can

feel the mundane world drawing me
back.

I pull my hand away and take a deep breath. I seem to be able to hold sway over my visions more and more, and they are no longer terrifying to me. Maybe that has more to do with my desire for peace than control of the visions. I'm sure I'll see Mom after she's judged favorably and has made her way to the Field of Reeds. To see her on Earth again would make my heart glow with warmth. Only the bas of the blessed dead can make the journey back to their tombs, reoccupy their bodies and walk again in the mundane world with their loved ones for the day, to go-forth-by-day. I don't know how much of this part of the mythology it true. Knowing a thing or two about physics and chemistry, it's hard to imagine or believe, but I do believe she will visit me in an incorporeal sense when she's ready.

It's stopped snowing, and the sky is clearing. As I leave the cemetery, the dark blue and orange evening sky makes me think that this could be the dawn of a new day, the beginning of a brighter future. But still I can't escape the feeling I'm standing on a knife's edge and that my life could come down on either side of it.

With the thoughts of ending my life sporadically coming and going, I drive to my dad's work to pick him up at the end of the day. I wonder if he even knows what he's done by banning me from seeing Belinda. I don't understand why it's so important to him who I'm friends with. He must really hate me.

The drive home is spent mostly in silence, with neither of us barely saying a word.

"How did your counseling session go?" Dad tries, but I'm not in the mood to talk.

I glance over at him and wonder whether William ever speaks to Dad about me. I wonder if William told him about Ramsi.

As we pass Belinda's, I look down her driveway and wonder what she's doing. The lights are all on in her house. It's only been a day and I already miss her. Dread rises from the pit of my stomach when I think about having to tell her I can't see her anymore – the thought floors me and makes me feel sick to my stomach.

When we arrive home, I glance at my Mustang, where it is still parked in the garage. I look at the engine and shake my head. I'm never going to finish it now. I guess I'll have to return Warren's engine stand and hoist some time.

The Mustang has its boot hanging out of the garage with the roller door lowered to the foot of the rear window. With no engine, the front of the car sits several inches higher than it normally would. I can't look at it anymore.

I head to my room and spend some time reading *The Egyptian Book of the Dead* on the end of my bed. I'm starting to understand her journey in detail, and I find this comforting. I'm no longer afraid of my visions and look forward to them. They are a momentary escape from reality. All I want to do is escape this world and live in a metaphysical one where anything is possible.

I suspect that the reason why I appear as Anubis in my visions is because of my deep desire to protect my mom, something I couldn't do on Earth. Or maybe it's because I really am Anubis. Maybe that's why I survived the crash.

I open the box for my new medication and crack out a pill. Maybe third times the charm. I gulp it down with a glass of water and climb into bed.

I spend the entire day reading, which is all that I can bring myself to do, and I'm still lying in bed when Dad returns home. I watch his shadow under my door as he walks down the hall. It's nearly eight o'clock, so I wait for him to have his shower and head to the living room, where he'll likely watch TV until midnight.

After my shower, the mirror over the vanity is slightly fogged, so I wipe it and start brushing my teeth.

As I study my distorted reflection in the foggy mirror, the horrifying image of me opening up my carotid artery with a knife and blood rushing down my neck explodes in my mind, unbidden and from apparently nowhere. I gasp, dropping my toothbrush in the sink, but instead of hearing the soft patter of plastic bouncing around in the sink, I hear the sound of steel on porcelain, reflecting my mind's eye.

Raw emotions flood my body. Pain and depression take over. I ball my hands into fists and lean against the vanity. I'm in agony, like my whole body's being crushed from the outside while exploding from the inside. I have an overwhelming urge to end this madness right now. Closing my eyes, I try hard not to burst into tears.

I spit out the last of the toothpaste and take a deep whimpering breath, trying to clear my mind. *What the hell was that?* Why has my depression gotten so much worse all of a sudden? I didn't think that was even possible. I think back over the past couple of days. Could it be from trudging up those painful, long-lost memories of Ramsi? Is it from being cut off from Belinda? Being all alone again is for sure making my depression worse, but this is something altogether different.

It must be the new antidepressants. It has to be. I rush to my room and grab my medication, and when I return to the bathroom, I flush them all down the toilet. I gasp again, shaking my head. I'm so fatigued from this fight with depression. In the darkness of my mind, a silent war is being waged. And it's one I feel I'm about to lose.

Chapter 14

With the darkest hours behind us, Khepri's future is secure, but not entirely guaranteed. For Seth, God of Deserts, who laps up corruption, lies in wait of this hour of the night. Seth and his associates will stop at nothing to defeat Horus, to prove that it is Seth that should rule over Egypt. The contendings of Horus and Seth have seen many great battles come to pass. Ever since Seth ate lettuce tainted with Horus' semen, Seth has fought without honor and will stop at nothing for vengeance. It is a senseless rivalry, for my father Osiris, Foremost of the Westerners, will surly never let either leave the Duat and return to the mundane world. Only through trickery could one escape, and who would be so foolish to trick Osiris?

The Mesektet flows forward on the waters of Nun. The air is calm.

Shani joins me by my side.

"O Lord Anubis, when will we arrive at the Hall of the Two Truths?"

I break my stare from the waters and look upon her face. "The Osiris Shani, it is not far. For the eastern akhet is just beyond – the eastern junction between the subterranean and celestial spheres where Ra is reborn."

"Will we see Tomorrow, the great lion of the east?"

"If you are found innocent in the Hall of the Two Truths, if your shabti works for you in the Field of Reeds, and if you are found worthy to become an akh in the celestial sphere, then all of these things will come to pass before you."

"O Lord Anubis, I do wish for these things, to be with the gods as an imperishable star."

I smile.

A hissing comes for the waters of Nun. I make haste for the prow. Ahead, a hippopotamus – its rounded ears and monstrous head above water – is swimming toward us at great speed.

"I don't understand, how can anything survive in the waters of Nun?"

"The Osiris Shani, stand back. It is Seth, God of Deserts. Cruel, malicious, and fierce is he."

In the form of a hippopotamus, Seth opens his giant jaws wide and crashes into the bow of the bark. We brace quickly before we come to a sudden stop. I grab Shani to pull her in close.

From the stern of the bark, Horus transforms into a sun-disk with wings. We bake in the heat of the intense light as he flies overhead, his flaming falcon wings roar as they thud the air over and over.

Once over the water, he swoops down, driving Seth from the waters of Nun. Seth lets out a thunderous roar that rolls across the sky as Horus swoops again and again.

Seth runs ashore, chased by Horus and his radiant heat and blinding light.

Thoth quickly runs to the steering oar and directs the bark toward land, where a lone sycamore tree stands, and we watch as Seth transforms into his normal form: a man with the head of an oppugnant beast, with a long, curved snout, large ears, and skin like black granite. He carries a was scepter in one hand and an ankh – the symbol of immortality and life – in the other.

Horus swoops down and flares his wings, also transforming into his normal form. With the head of a falcon, he wears a fish-scale pattern vest and a kilt with a bull's tail. He whirls his was scepter through the air as he prepares for battle.

Horus and Seth face-off with was scepters in hand and feet spread.

"Anubis, should we help?" Shani asks.

I shake my head. "Horus does not need our help, for he commands the army of the blessed dead."

Horus plants his was scepter in the ground and the earth quakes. A monstrous rumble carries through the air. From the east, the clanking of weapons and shields, and thousands of marching feet can be heard. Dust rises into the sky as the army nears. Thousands of warriors armed with swords, daggers, and javelins, and protected therewith shields march in unison, their flesh rejuvenated by the presence of Khepri. It is the greatest army to ever march across Egypt, and in the afterlife, a powerful and honorable band of men prepared to die a second death. They march to a stop behind Horus, and silence falls over the land.

Likewise, Seth plants his was scepter in the ground, and the air twists and turns in a storming wind. A great sandstorm blows in – the Sands of the Necropolis – from west to east. Sokar, one of Seth's many accomplices, in the form of a falcon, precedes the dust storm. Soaring high in the sky, he scouts ahead as he leads his army. The storming wind halts, and the sand falls to the ground, revealing the army of the damned. Decaying meat hangs from the skeletons, which are covered in maggots and loose mummy bandages. Holding axes, spears, and knives, they stand, tortured and weary.

The Duat falls deathly silent.

From the gunwale of the Mesektet, Thoth bows his ibis head toward Horus. Horus lifts his was scepter and charges toward Seth, screaming a terrifying war cry, his ba filled therewith bravery. His army of blessed dead warriors charge, filling the air with dust, and seconds later, the sound of steel clanking, mashing, and grinding fills the Duat.

The army tears through Sokar's, laying them unto dust.

In the center of the battle, Seth and Horus contest for supremacy as they have many times before. Their was scepters crash together in a battle of strength. One of Sokar's maggoty soldiers tackles Seth, blindsiding him, and brings them both crashing to the ground. Horus rolls to his side, grabs his was scepter and cracks it over the maggoty soldier's back, turning him into dust.

Another soldier tries the same move, but Horus trips him. He lies cowering on the sandy desert ground as Horus approaches. The soldier pleads for his life as he tries to crab away. Horus reaches down and effortlessly pulls the soldier into the air by the ankle. As the soldier arcs over his head, Horus pulls down with all his might and the soldier hits the ground so hard his maggoty body is swallowed by the sandy ground. And like that, he vanishes from existence.

Sokar swoops down with his talons outstretched, clawing at Horus, who beats him off with his was scepter. Seth launches another attack; Horus blocks him and pushes him back before grabbing his was scepter by the end, whirling it around and drawing down from the sky like an axe. Horus breaks Seth's was scepter and cracks him over the head. He falls backward unconscious.

Horus plants his was scepter into the ground and rips out his knife from its sheath. The shiny steel blade and gold handle glint in the light of Khepri.

I pull Shani toward me in protection as we watch from the gunwale, for I know of that which Horus is about to do.

He lifts Seth's kilt and cuts off his testicles, casting them aside. Seth jolts awake and sees his testicles lying in the dirt. Screaming, he rises to his feet, throws his was scepter away and charges toward Horus like a deranged beast. They wrestle for a second, but the unbridled rage in

Seth overpowers Horus. Seth grabs Horus' falcon head with both hands, and using his thumbs, he gauges his eyes, rendering him blind.

In a godly, bellowing voice, Thoth yells, "Halt!"

The silence that follows makes my blood run cold and causes Shani to look up at me in fright.

Sokar's army has been decimated, with Sokar nowhere to be seen, while Horus and Seth kneel on the ground with nothing left with which to fight. The remaining army of the damned turns unto dust and falls upon the land. Shani and I watch as the army of blessed dead warriors regroup and march east.

That is when we notice that Seth has gone. One minute he was kneeling by Horus' side; the next, he's nowhere to be seen. The shapeshifter no doubt ran away like the coward that he is.

Horus limps back, blind, toward the Mesektet. He fought well, honorably; it is indeed an honor to have him in Khepri's entourage – a worthy ruler of Egypt if ever I saw one.

"Thoth, what is your call?" I ask, as he is the ultimate judge of such contendings.

"Horus, God of the Sky," Thoth rules. "He fights for Egypt with integrity and stands as a defender unto Ra and Osiris."

By the time Horus reaches the shore, Hathor, Lady of the West, has magically appeared. She is in the form of a woman and wears a long red dress, cow horns, and a sun-disk. In her hand she carries a jug of gazelle milk.

"Horus," she says in a soft motherly voice. "Allow me to treat your wounds."

Horus stumbles toward the sound of her voice. With his arms outstretched, he places a hand on Hathor's shoulder. "I am blind, Hathor. The languid one did this unto me."

"Fear not, my dear. Tilt your head to one side."

Horus does as he's asked, and Hathor pours the gazelle milk over his face. Horus gasps as Hathor takes away her jug, blinking away the excess milk and wipes his face. "O Hathor, I can see once more."

Hathor smiles and Horus hugs her.

As Horus boards the Mesektet, Thoth is standing in the prow frantically flicking through the Book of Thoth.

"What is wrong?" I ask as we move to crowd around him.

He turns to us, and we see that all the color in his face has drained. "Someone has stolen pages from my book."

Isis gasps. "O Thoth, of which pages do thou speak?"

"I cannot be certain until I can compare this book with its double in the Hall of the Two Truths."

Aya's and Eman's hearts, the clay from the Lake of Natron, and now this ... Who could be behind it all?

"O Nephthys," I ask my birth mother, "this is Seth's realm, could he be behind the theft?"

"Anubis, my son, in the Duat, anything is possible. We will not stop seeking the answer to the question of what purpose these thefts have."

Isis and I lock eyes. "O Isis, it troubles my heart, for I should be doing more to put an end to this theft. They stole the pages right from under us."

"Thou are not to blame, for they have deceived us all," Isis says. "I will speak therewith Osiris, Foremost of the Westerners, and we shall bring the languid one to their knees. Now, we must all disembark and accompany the Osiris Shani to the Hall of the Two Truths, to her judgement."

I bow toward her. I believe she and my father will stop this treachery before the night is out.

I take Shani's hand. "The Osiris Shani, the time has come for us to disembark. To the Hall of the Two Truths I will take you; your innocence you must declare."

Shani bows. "O Lord Anubis, I am ready."

I wait for everyone to walk down the gangplank and go to my half-brother. "Horus, I will see you at the eastern akhet."

Horus bows toward me and places his hand on my shoulder. "I will maintain vigilance as I ferry Khepri eastward. I will wait for you in the east, and I hope to see the Osiris Shani again before this night is out."

I join the others who are now standing by the sycamore tree.

Shani looks up. "O Lord Anubis, will I get to see the majesty of the rebirth of Ra, as Khepri the dawn sun?"

"Horus will ferry the Mesektet eastward, and when Khepri reaches the eastern akhet, all in the Field of Reeds will bathe in his glory."

Shani's face lights with a broad smile.

Chapter 15

I've spent the entire day in bed, with no energy to do anything, just watching my alarm clock as the hours tick by – time has lost all meaning. I am wishing for this mundane life to just end. I begin to picture a world, one in which I don't exist. Would that world be any different to this one? Would Dad even care if I died?

There's a knock at the door. Five o'clock. I lie still, wondering if there's any point in getting up, but then there's another *rat-a-tat-tat*.

That's Belinda.

I turn my blanket down and crawl out of bed, my head fuzzy and sore. I'm so tired, I don't even know whether I can string a sentence together.

I open the front door.

When Belinda sees me, she gasps. "You look terrible! Why haven't I seen you?" she asks, frowning heavily.

I'm on the edge of breaking into tears. I can't think of anything to say. I just swallow.

"Why weren't you at school today?"

The thought of telling her everything crashes around in my head and I take a deep, stuttered breath.

"How long has it been since you've slept?"

I try to do the math – twenty ... four, forty-eight plus nine – but my mind just locks up, numb. "I don't know ... three days?" I manage to croak.

Belinda looks shocked.

"Don't you want to hang out anymore?" she asks. She looks like she's on the verge of breaking into tears herself.

I shake my head. Damn it, I didn't mean to do that or make her think that I don't want to see her. My mind is so jumbled I can't think straight.

"Why not?" she asks, tears hanging from her eyes.

"You wouldn't understand," I say, giving up. Even if Dad allowed me to see her, she'll inevitably leave me one day.

A tear streaks down her cheek. My heart breaks seeing it, and I feel sick in the pit of my stomach.

She steps back, before turning and running off.

I whisper as she starts up our driveway, "Belinda."

She slows to a fast walk and looks over her shoulder, almost as if hoping she'll catch a glimpse of me chasing after her. I think about running after her, but it's too late. I've just made a huge mistake.

She turns to continue walking away from me.

"Anput," I whisper instinctively.

She stops and looks back at me.

I know Belinda is my soulmate now, and not just from this world, but from the Duat too. We stare into each other's teary eyes from afar.

Belinda whispers back. I follow the shape her mouth forms, and I'm sure it matches what I thought I heard.

"Anubis."

Did she really just say that?

She's too far away for me to have heard. Did I just imagine her lips moving? The fact that she stopped and turned around when I called her Anput could have just been a coincidence, but I'm certain I heard her call me by my true name.

She turns and storms off up our driveway.

Tears streak down my face. When Belinda's out of sight, fear floods my body – I'm worried that this could be the last time I ever see her. I close the door, lean my forehead against it and whimper. I can't believe I just told her I didn't want to see her again. I'll be alone forever.

Damn my feeble mind. Damn this world.

I walk into the kitchen, sit down and bury my face into my palms.

I'm so tired, nothing makes sense anymore. I look around the empty house, feeling completely alone once again, and decide I need to get out of here. It's still too early to pick up Dad, so I decide to visit Mom's grave. I may as well make the most of having Dad's truck.

When I stop at the top of our driveway, I have second thoughts. It can't be safe to be driving so tired. I don't care so much what happens to me, but I'd kill myself if I hurt someone else in an accident. I think back to the poor truck driver and feel an understanding.

The drive to the cemetery is like some kind of strange time warp, and before I know it, I'm already here. I don't even remember pulling out of the driveway or turning off our road.

My head is throbbing, and I'm not sure if I can handle seeing into the Duat right now. As I kneel on the grass, my heart is aching, and I start to cry. I'm becoming so unraveled. I wish I could see Mom go-forth-by-day, to see her on Earth once more.

But my visions are the only thing still connecting me to her, so I reach out and touch her tombstone ...

Standing before the portal of onyx and gold, I stare at its black ink-like surface, unsure who's reflection I'll see. My normal human face slowly becomes clearer. My hands are also normal. Why in these visions am I human, why not Anubis?

Something flies past me swiftly. I can feel the shifting movement of air as it passes, and I hear a strange sound, like that of air escaping giant lungs. Anubis, still in his shadowy form with ribbon-like tentacles, circles above. He descends, getting closer and closer, slowing his dizzying circles until he reaches me.

He stops at chest height, his tentacles waving in the air like wings. I go to speak, but as soon as I open my mouth, he charges toward me. I step back as he flies straight into my chest. I gasp in shock and look behind me, but he's nowhere to be seen. He went into me.

Some kind of sixth sense directs me back to the portal, and I look at my reflection. I see myself changed. Now with the head of a jackal, my hands and forearms are covered in fur.

I'm Anubis, just like all my other visions.

I run my giant fur-covered hands over my face. My heart hammers, yet at the same time I feel at peace. Like this is where I belong.

Everything goes black for a second, and when the light returns, I'm suddenly standing on the Mesektet, traveling toward the eastern akhet. Thoth is standing in the prow reading his book. I look to my left to find Anput standing by my side.

She suddenly twists her neck and looks me right in the eye, her stare boring straight into my soul. "Anubis," she says.

I pull my hand away from Mom's tombstone, my heart pounding, and muddle through what I just saw. I connect it to all of the other visions I've had of being Anubis in the Duat.

I'm certain now, more than ever, that I am Anubis.

The exact meaning of my visions still eludes me, but my identity I know in my heart to be true. And I believe in time, the full meaning will be revealed, for it's only time that separates the living from the dead. I wonder whether my depression is a side effect of being Anubis; he is, after all, a god of the necropolis.

I can feel the temptation to cut myself out of this mundane world and return to the Duat where I belong, but a thought stops me: maybe I, Anubis, have been sent back to Earth for some grander purpose.

After only getting a couple of hours of sleep, I crawl out of bed and stare at my alarm clock in a zombie-like trance. *Damn, I feel like crap.* There's no way I'm going to school today.

I head out to the kitchen and stand in front of the fireplace, taking in the heat. My head is aching. I feel like I did the day after Mom died: chewed up and spat out, and depressed as all hell.

My depression is a demon living within, lurking in the shadows, destroying my soul. I know I have to kill it before it kills me, and I know it will be a fight to the death, but how do I defeat a metaphysical demon that resides within my mind?

I've seen Khepri and Selket defeat Apophis, so I know demons can be slain, but the difference is: Khepri had help. How am I supposed to defeat my demon alone? All my visions of the Duat have been from a single night, and this can only mean one thing: my time is running out.

I get dressed and then go into Dad's room, to the nightstand on his side of the bed. I slide out the top drawer and feel at the very back, where a dark gray lockbox sits inconspicuously in the shadows. I pull it out and turn the key. Inside, is a nickel-plated snub-nosed thirty-eight revolver, six brass rounds at the ready. I pick it up by the checkered walnut handle and feel the cold steel's weight. I stare at it. What to do next?

To hell with him!

Leaving the lockbox where I found it, I tuck the thirty-eight into the back of my jeans and pull my shirt and jumper down to conceal it.

Outside, my breath mists the air. It's only morning and just above freezing. The ground is still splotched with snow, but it has already melted off the trees, exposing the dark bark and leafless branches.

I follow the dirt track down to the back of our property and sit on a dead rotten log. I pull out the gun. The cold steel weighs down my hands.

My mind feels like it's frozen, static, and empty. I slide my index finger over the trigger and feel a sense of power – with this, there are so many possibilities. I aim the gun at a tree and pull the trigger. The shot rings out and my hands snap back from the recoil. The smell of burned gunpowder fills the frigid air.

Adrenaline has awakened my mind, but it feels decoupled from my body. I have no foresight as to what happens next, like my mind could decide one thing, but my body does another. I take aim again and let three shots off this time. My ears ring. Two more shots in rapid succession and the gun is empty. I wrap my hand around the revolver's cylinder and feel the warmth. It's like an Island of Fire in my hand.

A light wind howls through the needles of the conifers. There are no bird calls, no voices or any other sounds. I could be a million miles from anywhere, or the last person on Earth. I picture the waters of Nun flowing through the Duat and imagine what it would feel like to fall into them, what it's like to drown, to not exist.

I spend the rest of the day in bed, staring out the window. At five o'clock, an hour earlier than usual, I hear Dad pull into the garage. *What the?* There's no way he could know about his revolver ... I sit up and anxiously wait for him to walk down the hall. He pauses at my closed door briefly before continuing, and I lie back down, my head throbbing, tired to the point of utter exhaustion.

A minute later there are three enormous thumps on my door. "Kyle!" he hollers.

Shit, I knew I should have reloaded his gun. He probably smelled the burned gunpowder.

I crawl out of bed and open the door. "What?"

He looks like he's about to deck me. "I got a phone call from the Hodges today saying they heard gunshots. Care to explain why my revolver's got six spent cartridges in it?"

I shrug. "I was bored ... If you didn't want me using it, you should have locked it away properly instead of just leaving it in your draw where I—"

"This isn't about me," he screams so loud it hurts my ears. "If I ever catch you using my revolver again, watch out!" He takes a breath and then continues, "Your school called too ... you haven't been in for the past two days? Why the hell not?"

I open my mouth to speak but can't bring myself to tell him why. Instead, I slam my door, being careful not to slam it too hard that he'll open it again to shout at me. I can hear him in the hall breathing heavy.

Once I've recomposed myself, I think about how stupid I was with Belinda. I can't believe I told her I didn't want to see her anymore. My heart aches, and I collapse onto my bed, still gripped with depression.

I'm so sick of this world. Why does everything have to be so hard?

The following morning when I wake, I feel like death warmed up. Being off my medication has left me feeling extremely vulnerable, like anything could bring me to my knees. There is no way I'm going to school; I hate that place as much as I now hate being home. This will be my third day off school; Dad will hit the roof when he finds out – not that I care about anything at this point. All I want to do is run away and never come back.

My line of sight gravitates to my trashcan beside my desk, and I am reminded about the black powder I stashed in there. I open the top of the trashcan and pull out the bag, revealing the second bag I had hidden beneath it. There's still well over ten pounds left.

Time to unleash my destructive side – my dark side, the side that could ultimately bring Mom and I together again.

I head out to the kitchen to pick up an empty coffee tin, which is sitting next to the trash. It's the perfect size and would make an excellent canister for a bomb. I take it back to my room to fill it with roughly two pounds of black powder. I scan my room, not wanting to use a traditional wick, and my gaze finally settles on my torch. *Bingo.* I pick it up and remove the globe. Now all I have to find is some electrical cord and do some soft soldering.

An hour later the bomb's finished, and I stuff it into my backpack.

I walk down the trail to the back of our property, where I fired the gun, feeling an even greater sense of power, now I have the bomb in my backpack. The adrenaline coursing through my veins has drawn me out of the sleepless, catatonic state I've been stuck in for weeks – I finally feel alive again.

I also feel a vulnerability, that the bomb could go off at any moment. This knowledge only adds to my adrenaline. Maybe today will be the day I reenter the Duat and take up my true purpose as shepherd and protector of the dead ...

I choose a spot in the ground in front of a boulder, which I can use for protection, and then I begin to dig a big hole. Although it's spring, the dirt is freezing and hard work to dig with my hands. I place the bomb in the hole and unwind the electrical cord coming out of the coffee tin that's now wound in duct tape, like mummy bandages. I wonder what it would be like to detonate it right now. It's not like anyone would miss me, not even Belinda cares about me anymore. I wonder whether I would feel anything. Being Anubis, it probably wouldn't even kill me. *Maybe I'm immortal and that's why I survived the accident?*

I place the electrical cord around the boulder and lead the cable further back into the woods as far as it will go.

I get the nine-volt battery out of my pocket, and my heart is pounding as I connect the wires to the battery.

I wait.

Nothing.

Crap. What do I do now? Investigate to see what went wrong? Maybe the electrical cord came loose. Not keen to dig it out, I try again. My heart feels like a series of small explosions in my chest. I try again, leaving the battery connected longer this time.

Boom!

The thud is like nothing I've ever experienced, like someone just kicked me in the chest. It's ten times louder than the cannon. The boom rolls across the sky for a good ten seconds, just like thunder. I squint through the dust and rocks that rain from the sky. My ears are ringing, and I have an instant splitting headache.

I pick myself up and walk around to where I planted the bomb, but it's now a giant smoldering crater.

"That was heavy duty," I say to myself.

I kneel before the crater and clutch the soil. Feeling it run through my fingers, I wonder if the explosion could be heard in the Duat, in the subterranean sphere. Maybe if I blow a big enough hole in the ground, I can find another way into the Daut apart from killing myself. I'm desperate for change, any change, I don't care how it comes.

It's Friday, and after spending the whole week at home, I'm returning to the house after going for a walk when I spot Dad's truck in the garage. *What's he doing home?* It's only lunchtime. We haven't spoken since our huge fight over the gun, and he's stopped pushing me to go to school. I don't know what's going through his head, but, like me, I suspect he just doesn't care anymore.

I duck under the roller door of the garage and enter the kitchen, wondering where he is, and why he's home so early.

He's sitting on a stool, staring at me.

Now what? That's when I see my trashcan sitting on the bench, as is the rest of the black powder in its plastic bag.

Oh crap.

He hands me the local newspaper. The title reads: *Police investigate explosion on Conifer Crescent.*

"Are you insane?" he says, and then looks away, pursing his lips, as if, almost for a second, he regrets his choice of words. He turns back and tries again. "What were you thinking?"

I just stand there with no energy to argue.

He grasps his temples. "Do you know how much trouble you could have got in if the police caught you?" he yells, but it's not as loud as when he told me off for using his gun. "You can kiss any chance of going to university goodbye if you get a criminal record."

I shrug. That's a joke. Has he even seen my grades?

"Kyle." He shakes his head and lowers his voice. "I don't have the energy anymore." He picks up the plastic bag and hands it to me. "Take it out the back and burn it."

I feel bad for seeing him so distraught. I take the bag from him, unsure what to say.

"Look, Kyle, I know I'm not the world's best dad, but we can't keep going on like this. I know I need to be a better father ..." His voice trails off as if he's struggling to find the words. "I don't know how we got to this point."

"I do," I say, feeling a mix of emotions: fury, sympathy ... "You're never around."

I'm surprised by his retaliatory expression; it's not one of anger but sadness, as though he agrees.

He nods. "I know. The truth is ... I don't know how to be a better father. I grew up dirt poor, and I guess I've always thought that if I worked hard and provided for my family, you'd have a better life ... that we'd have a better life. But it turns out I'm no better at parenting than my father was."

I'm surprised at his honesty. He's never opened up about his childhood before. I know so little about that part of his life.

"How has your depression been?" he asks.

"Not good," I say. It's a severe understatement, but I don't know what else to say.

There's an awkward silence, and I don't know what to do. We're both in uncharted territory. *Should I tell him more?*

"William says that ties with the community and having a plan for the future are important," I say. I hope that he'll see the hint about Belinda in my words.

Dad nods in silent contemplation. "Will you go to school next week?" he asks softly.

I nod.

The past couple of weeks have been a living hell with the lines between my two worlds blurred. I don't even think my life in the Duat is this hard, this dark. Maybe, like they say, it's always darkest before dawn. I've always thought that that saying was a little stupid, but now, I pray it's true – I don't think I can go on like this for much longer.

Chapter 16

Walking toward the eastern akhet, with Shani between Anput and me, each of us holding her hands, we can see the sacred Hall of the Two Truths. Thoth and Isis are walking side by side, and Nephthys is further ahead. Shani spots the sacred hall and looks up at me, unable to hide her concern.

I stop and get down on one knee. "The Osiris Shani, when we enter the Hall of the Two Truths, remember, speak from the heart, and heard you will be."

Shani swallows. "O Lord Anubis, my fate lies in wait. I have released my burden of guilt ... but ..."

"The Osiris Shani," I say, clasping her hand, "I feel guilt for not chasing down the languid one who would steal, but just because one feels guilt, does not mean they are guilty."

Shani nods, her frown slowly subsiding.

"Are you ready?" I ask.

"I am."

We climb the limestone steps to the Hall of the Two Truths. Shani stops when we reach the top, and she pivots her head skyward. I follow her stare. High above us soars Maat, Goddess of Truth, Morality, and Justice. With her wings spread wide, she glides down toward us, her features slowly becoming discernible as she descends – the beautiful figure of a woman with giant wings of green and blue plumage.

"O Lord Anubis, it is Maat. Is she here to oversee the ceremony?"

"Indeed, the Osiris Shani."

As she glides toward us, she flares her giant wings, slowing dramatically. A couple of vigorous thuds of the air and she lands gracefully on the steps before us. She folds her wings in behind her back and walks up the stairs. Her long, elegant red dress accentuates her curves.

"O Lord Anubis, the Osiris Shani, it is time," Maat says, looking each of us in the eye.

I look down at Shani, who has a glowing smile. Taking her hand, I lead her toward the entrance of the Hall of the Two Truths.

Inside, we walk to the center of the cylindrical audience chamber. With blue, turquois, and brown columns, there are pairs of uraei – erect golden cobras –

and feathers of Maat running along a limestone shelf near the roof. Above us sit forty-two gods – the council of the Hall of the Two Truths – on a balcony that wraps around the chamber.

"The Osiris Shani, face the first god of the council and declare your innocence," I say, gesturing with an open palm.

Shani does as I asked and swallows before saying to the first god, "I have done no wrong."

The god bows toward Shani, an acceptance of her declaration.

She turns to the second. "I have not robbed."

The second god bows also.

Shani swallows hard as she faces the third. "I have not stolen."

The third god stares at Shani. He steps down off his throne, and Shani grabs my hand in fright.

"Shani, you declared your innocence, but you are conflicted," he says in a deep voice, stopping to kneel in front of her.

Shani freezes.

He reaches out and into the chest of Shani's ba, his hand disappearing beyond her dress. A short moment later, he removes his hand. "The Osiris Shani, I have held your heart and know your truth. You have not stolen. You may pass."

Shani continues to declare her innocence, and after she has spoken to the forty-second god of the council, a glorious smile comes over her face. In the least, her fate, as I have known all along, will be that of the bas that reside in the Field of Reeds. At best, she will join the gods in the celestial sphere as an akh.

We leave the cylindrical audience chamber and enter Osiris' audience chamber – the place some people fear.

Over the archway is a statue of Sokar, recumbent in mummiform, flanked by uraei. The walls of the audience chamber are green-striped limestone. In the very center are the great scales and the bas of Aya, Eman, and Tau waiting to be judged. I do not know why Tau would even show his face here, even if he had nothing to do with the theft of this night, he will still surely fail his judgement. Behind the scales, offerings of bread, beer, oxen, and foul sit on an offering slab.

Osiris, Foremost of the Westerners, my father, sits upon a great throne of gold, turquoise, jasper, and emerald; at its base are gold double-leaf doors.

Shani's face lights up when she sees him. Bandaged from neck to toe in fish-scale pattern bandages, only his green hands and face are visible. Wearing a white atef-crown – the double-plume ostrich feathers of the vindicated King of Upper and Lower Egypt – he holds a shepherd's crook, was scepter, and flagellum. Behind him stands his sister-wife, Isis.

Thoth stands to the right of the scales. With the head of an ibis, he also wears a nemes headdress, a white sash across his chest, and a kilt. With a scribal pallet in one hand and a reed brush in the other, he stands tall, ready to record events.

Ammit, Swallower of the Dead, sits on a reed mat to the left of the scales. She's the most hideous of demons, with the head of a crocodile, a lion's torso, and the hindquarters of a hippopotamus.

Shani takes one look at her, steps back and clasps my hand tight.

"The Osiris Shani, you have naught to fear." I try to comfort her.

In single file, the members of the Great Tribunal enter the audience chamber from the rear and stand on another limestone balcony, overlooking the great scales.

Shani clasps my hand even tighter.

The sound of several great thuds of air fills the room, and Shani and I spin around. Maat has taken flight and is rising rapidly toward the roof. When she reaches the ceiling, she transforms – becoming one with the roof – into a beautiful, colored mural of herself. From there, she will oversee the weighing of the heart ceremony. In a seated position, her wings are outstretched, spanning most of the roof, as she looks down upon us.

I look at Shani, who is clearly in awe of the magnificent painting.

"The Osiris Shani, wait here, for I am the guardian of the scales and have a duty to perform."

Shani lets go of my hand and steps closer to Anput.

I walk past Tau and approach Aya and Eman at the head of the short line. They, like Shani, all await their judgements.

"Anubis," Osiris shouts in a bellowing voice. "What is the meaning of this? Aya and Eman have passed already of this night."

I gasp. "What?"

"Just a moment ago, as supreme judge, I granted them access to the Field of Reeds."

I recall the theft of their hearts, the clay from the Lake of Natron, and the pages from the Book of Thoth. "Thoth, can you check what pages were stolen from your book?"

Thoth hurriedly flicks through the Book of Thoth that had pages stolen from it and then its duplicate that he keeps in the Hall of the Two Truths. "They are transformative spells."

Isis and I lock eyes. To confirm my suspicion, I look into the chest cavities of Aya and Eman's bas, where their hearts should be. "These are the real Aya and Eman, for their hearts are missing."

Isis steps out from behind Osiris. "That is the purpose of the thefts of this night. The pages from the Book of Thoth were used to breathe life into clay forms of Aya and Eman by using clay from the Lake of Natron therewith Aya's and Eman's hearts. The two that have already passed are imposters."

"Who would do such a thing?" I say, staring Tau in the eye. We never found any evidence, but I'm sure he's tied up in this somehow.

Osiris leans back in his throne, deep in thought. "Who would use such trickery and deceit? Only the most wicked would dare cross me."

"Osiris," Isis says, "the night is not out. After we judge the real Aya and Eman who stand before you, we will find the culprits and bring them before thou."

"And I will smite them from existence!" Osiris thunders.

"Father, shall we continue with the weighing of the hearts?"

Osiris bows toward me.

I go to Aya and Eman, kneel and bow my head. "The Osiris Aya, the Osiris Eman, I am filled therewith sorrow and guilt, for your hearts have been stolen."

"O Lord Anubis," Aya says, "your sorrow is shared but please feel no guilt, for we know it was not you. Our bodies have been buried with heart scarabs. Will you use these instead?"

They each pull out a heart scarab carved from green jasper. My heart rejoices. Heart scarabs such as these, on the rare occasions that something should happen to the deceased's own heart, can be weighed against the feather of Maat instead.

"The Osiris Aya, the Osiris Eman, of course you may use your heat scarabs."

Aya removes her heart scarab from around her neck and holds it out with both hands. She places it into my palm with care.

I position the scarab on the left pan of the great scales of onyx and gold, which is adorned with a golden baboon.

Thoth hands me the feather of Maat, which I place on the right pan.

Kneeling next to the scales, I pull the pin to unlock them and allow them to discover the truth. As expected, the feather of Maat is heavier than Aya's heart scarab. Aya and Eman rejoice as Thoth records the events.

"The Osiris Aya, the vindicated, your heart has been judged before the Great Tribunal and it has not created opposition against you. To Osiris, I will lead you shortly."

Aya stands to the side, with tears of happiness glinting on her cheeks.

Eman hands me his heart scarab, and I place it on the scales. He, like Aya, is judged favorably, and they both stand together in relief and euphoria.

Tau's next in line; he steps forward, face drawn, jaw clenched.

Ammit stands in anticipation.

I get down on one knee. "Tau, will you permit me to take your heart so we can weigh it on the great scales?"

"I do," he says, his voice shaking.

I reach into Tau's ba, carefully take his heart and place it on the left pan, the feather of Maat on the right. Thoth and I lock eyes.

Sometimes you just know deep down when something is wrong.

Kneeling next to the scales, I pull out the pin to unlock them, and as soon as I do so, the left pan, which holds Tau's heart, plummets.

Ammit opens her jaws wide, exposing rows of sharp teeth, snatching Tau's heart from its place on the pan and swallows it whole.

Tau cries out in horror, almost like he was expecting a different result, and the limestone floor beneath him turns black. Ghostly black serpents rise out of the black floor and wrap themselves around his ankles and wrists, dragging him down. Amid harrowing screams, he disappears into the floor. His journey's not over, but soon enough it will be.

It is now time for Shani's fate. I beckon her forward.

Afraid and shaking, she steps toward the scales.

I get down on one knee. "The Osiris Shani, will you permit me to take your heart so we can weigh it on the great scales?"

"I do."

I reach into her ba and carefully remove her heart, before performing the weighing.

Shani's heart rises and the pan holding the feather of Maat falls.

Thoth records events, and Ammit sits on her hindquarters, with no need to take the heart as she did Tau's. I place Shani's heart back inside her ba. Her face is glowing with joy.

Anput and I lead Shani, Aya, and Eman to Osiris, where they place their offerings on the slab: Aya and Eman leave fowl and bread, while Shani has brought a bouquet of lilies and lotuses.

Kneeling, she raises her palms in adoration. "O Osiris, Foremost of the Westerners, I am grateful a million times true, to be in your kingdom, to dwell with the blessed dead."

Osiris bows, acknowledging her offering, and then speaks to the three. "Aya, Eman, and Shani, the vindicated, you may enter the Field of Reeds. Anubis and Anput will shepherd you as it is their will." Osiris looks me in the eye. "Anubis, my son, it is troubling that Aya's and Eman's hearts would be stolen. So many forms could have been created to tip the balance of power in the Duat. It concerns me greatly that someone would go to such lengths, only to create second forms of Aya and Eman. Search for the corrupt ones that would live on what is putrid. Stopped, they must be, for there is more to this deceit than what we behold."

I bow toward my father. "O Lord Osiris, I will find the guilty and return the Osiris Aya's and Eman's hearts, even if I have to destroy the languid one myself."

I take Shani's hand, while Anput does the same with Aya and Eman and leads them outside. "The Osiris Shani, the vindicated, come, for you are of the blessed dead in the Kingdom of Osiris."

She smiles broadly, her soul now free to enjoy the pleasures of the afterlife, and if she so wishes, return to her body in the mundane world for the day and be with her family once more, to go-forth-by-day.

Chapter 17

I arrive at William's office, half-asleep, not having slept in days. Being off my medication and with the huge fights Dad and I've been having, I feel like I've hit rock bottom. Plus, having been banned from seeing Belinda and with the pain of accidently telling her I don't want to see her, I can't imagine things getting any worse.

William sits on the couch and looks at me. "I know *that* face. You haven't been sleeping?"

I shake my head.

"How long's it been since you've slept?"

"Not sure ... two or three days."

William shakes his head. "The new medication's not working?"

I think back to the vision I had at the vanity when I was brushing my teeth and shake my head, again. I open my mouth, but my words stick to my tongue. I try again. "After starting them ... I was brushing my teeth one night ... and I had this really violent image explode in my head

... something I would never consider doing. It really floored me. I *literally* gasped. I flushed the pills down the toilet. Later, I guessed that the position of my toothbrush and the action was what triggered the image, my hand being near the carotid artery and all." By the time I finish, I have tears in my eyes. I wipe them away before they streak down my face.

"Oh ... I understand. I'm sorry you went through that. That can happen," William replies, looking distraught. "So, you've been off your medication all this time?"

I nod.

"You should have made another appointment and come to see me. You might not like to hear me phrase it like this ... but this is still a result. A negative result, but it means we can go in another direction. Would you be willing to try another antidepressant?"

I nod unenthusiastically, feeling like I'm on the edge.

"Have you had any *other* thoughts of self-harm?"

I nod, not wanting to talk about them.

"Do you have a plan?"

"No."

"Have you been seeing Belinda?"

I shake my head. "I didn't go to school last week, and I avoided her all this week at school. When I'm home ...

I'm so lonely and feel like such an outcast, all I want to do is end it all."

William reads my face, his own heavy with concern.

What's the point in living if you're dead inside?

"I'm at the end of my road," I say with a quiver in my voice.

"Then maybe you should learn how to fly?" William says with a cheeky grin.

When I chuckle, it feels like a blinding ray of sunlight breaking through a monstrous sky. "I like that … maybe I should become a pilot."

"Now you're talking!" William says. "See how perspective matters?"

My smile lasts only a short while and my depressed mood returns when the moment passes.

"Has your risk-taking escalated at all?"

I nod, hesitating to elaborate. "I built a really big bomb the other day. I set it off down the back of our property."

"That was you? I read about that in the paper." William raises his eyebrows and sits forward on his couch. "Do you think building bombs could be an attempt to get your father's attention?"

I feel the muscles in my face tug slightly. "Mission accomplished then."

"How's that? Did he work out it was you?"

"Yeah."

"Your behavior is definitely becoming increasingly self-destructive. People that suffer from depression often seek out risky and self-destructive behavior. Have you considered this might also be your way of trying to be with your mother again?"

I nod as a tear races down my face. I guess what he says is true; I know I don't care what happens to me, and it would be good to be with her again.

"I'm haunted by her memory, for what was, is now gone. Is it really better to have loved and lost?" I ask.

"In time, the pain will pass, and you'll remember your mother for the beautiful woman that she was, and your soul will be richer for it," William says. "Have you been to her grave since the funeral?"

I nod again, recalling the visions of the Duat.

"It still doesn't sound like you've gained closure. It's been over three months since the accident," William says in a soft voice. "Have you put any thought into how you're going to move on?"

I look him in the eye. His words feel like an attack, but deep down I know he's right. I'm suddenly overcome with grief and my hands start to shake. I burst into tears and bury my head in my palms. I picture Mom that day in the kitchen as she turned to face me, as she fitted her necklace with the feather of Maat amulet, and all the little moments at her funeral: the shabti and the golden eagle feather. I clench my fist to my chest. It's like my whole body is made of pain. All I want is to see her smiling face once more. The hard truth of it hits me like a lightning bolt; I'm never going to see here again – not in the mundane world at least. I'm looking forward to returning to the Duat so I can be with her once more.

"I don't want to live anymore," I cry.

A minute passes before I compose myself, my hands and face wet with tears. I pull a tissue out from the box on the coffee table and wipe my nose; my face feels like it's made of cement, and my head is throbbing. I glance up at William.

"I'm not supposed to talk to you so openly, but take it from me, these kinds of death spirals end in one of two ways. One of which is you disappear down the drain hole never to return," William says, pausing for a moment. Then he asks, "Can I tell you a story?"

I frown, curious, but usher him on.

"When I left school, I really wanted to help people. It may seem irrational, but I decided I could do that by joining the Army. I used to work as a psychiatrist treating returned soldiers. The thing is, while I had this deep desire to help people, I simply wasn't cut out for the darkness of the war stories the soldiers told me about. Suffering from secondary stress, I started drinking, was court marshaled for dereliction of duty – found not guilty – but it was the straw that broke the camel's back. I left the Army, my wife left me, and I continued my drinking until I hit an all-time low."

I study William's face, the heavy wrinkles crisscrossing his face; I know now that they reflect more than just old age.

William continues, "I was walking home from the pub early one morning when I came across a man standing on the handrail of a bridge. He was in tears and muttering to himself ... ready to jump."

I raise my eyebrows in surprise, wondering where this is going.

"I started talking to him and eventually convinced him to step down. It was like divine providence," William says, shaking his palms to the sky, looking up, as though somehow communicating with God. "Suddenly, I realized I could still help people. So, take it from me, I've been where you are, and I know the hopelessness and permanence that you're feeling. Keep in mind, even the darkest days are still just days, and all days must end. You won't *always* feel like this."

I shake my head. "I don't understand ... I felt like I was getting my life back together when suddenly, the ground beneath me disappeared."

"I'd say it's the combination of a negative reaction to the medication and your dad's harsh restrictions that have driven you to where you are right now."

Feeling completely exhausted, I mutter, "Why's it gotta be so hard?"

"To quote Richard Bach: 'The bond that links your true family is not one of blood, but of respect and joy in each other's life.' The relationship you and your mom had is proof of that. You and your dad may never be great friends, but keep in mind, there is only *one* of him. He can't be replaced. It's worth trying, no matter how hard, to mend your relationship with him. In the least, you may find a way to get along so that once you finish school, you can still be in one another's lives ... to some degree."

I nod.

"Have you thought about what you want to do after school?"

I shake my head softly, unable to imagine next week let alone the end of school.

"Will you do that for me?"

"Yeah," I say, meeting his gaze.

"The challenge for you is to not only find what you're passionate about, but where you'll fit in. It's no good wanting to be a fireman if you're scared of heights!"

I chuckle. I'm so sick of feeling ruined, but I like talking to William, the wise old mentor he is. I don't know where I'd be right now if I didn't have him to talk to. I feel like we have a strange bond, not a typical friendship, but something else. I guess sharing your innermost feelings with someone will do that. Thinking back to my visions, I wonder what William would say if I told him, and what would happen. Would they lock me up? Could things get any worse? No, that's not possible.

"What's on your mind?" William asks, scratching his beard.

"Oh," I say. I stare at the floor a moment before looking back up, my heart starting to race. "I ... I've been having visions of being Anubis in the Duat." I study his face intensely, trying to read his mind, but his expression doesn't give anything away. *Is he not shocked by this?*

"Anubis, he's a guardian of the dead, isn't he?" he asks, cocking his head to one side as though he's trying to dislodge a memory from one of our previous conversations.

I nod, staring at him, wanting to know what he's thinking. He's clearly deep in thought as I tell him about all the visions I've been having traveling on the Mesektet.

"Have your delusions jeopardized yours or others' safety?"

I shake my head and say, "Do you believe in a metaphysical world, in life after death?"

"I believe in heaven and of the soul," William says, before pausing for a second. Then he adds, "Can you tell the difference between the two worlds?"

I nod. "Yeah, but when I'm there, it feels real ... like that's my life ... where I'm supposed to be."

"How do your delusions come to you?" he asks.

Hearing him call them "delusions" makes me feel even more broken.

I shrug. "I don't know ... at first, it was whenever I was asleep, but now they're during the day too. It's like an hour of the night in the Duat seamlessly splices into events on Earth. It's not like I lose an hour on Earth … I don't think." There's an awkward silence, and then I add, "I borrowed a book from the library, as I was wondering if they're religious delusions."

"No, they can't be, because there're not idiosyncratic," he says. "Ancient Egyptian mythology *is* a religion, and we can't class everyone that hears the voice of God as delusionary."

"You're not surprised to hear I've been having delusions?" I ask.

"No, but I am concerned. I'm going to write another prescription. Hopefully, we'll have more success with this new antidepressant, and I'm going to prescribe something for those delusions of yours. I'm also adding some sleeping pills to help you get some rest," William says as he scribbles on his notepad. "Let me know straight away if your delusions become invasive, or if your depression gets any worse."

I nod as he hands me the script.

"It being Friday, you're not going out partying, are you?" he asks jokingly and with a twinkle in his eyes.

I shake my head, managing a smile.

"We'll get you through this, buddy," he says.

As we walk to the door, William says, "I would also like to speak to your father soon."

I turn back to face him, not keen on the idea of them talking. I don't want him to say anything to Dad about my delusions.

"He's here. Well, he should be," I say. "He *said* he was picking me up."

"Oh, excellent. Can you send him in?"

I hesitate before nodding.

William opens the door for me, and I see Dad sitting in his truck. I'm not looking forward to this. I knock on his window and he winds it down.

"William said he'd like to talk to you," I say.

He doesn't say a word, just nods as he climbs out and goes inside.

I pace back and forth while I wait for Dad to finish talking with William. I wonder what they're talking about. It is excruciating. Dad better not go off the deep end if he finds out about my delusions. If he does, I'll leave and never come back. Then again, maybe Dad is having delusions too. For all I know, Dad is Osiris, just as I am Anubis. Osiris had a hard time on Earth too.

Sick of pacing, I open the door to Dad's truck and climb in. I look at my watch. He's been in there for twenty minutes. But a few minutes later, I spot them inside, heading to the front door.

The driver's side door creaks open and Dad jumps in.

I look away and try hiding my face, but I can feel him looking at me. I swallow. "I've gotta go to the chemist."

A few seconds pass in silence.

When I finally look at him, I see his face is drawn. There is something heavy on his mind. I guess William told him everything. I'm just waiting for him to give me a hard time, to tell me I'm making it all up, that I just want to get some attention.

His chin flaps up and down a couple of times and his eyes are glassy. "I was wrong to stop you from seeing Belinda. I'm sorry. I didn't know her dad can't work."

My heart skips a beat. This rare show of emotion stuns me. The silence that follows is unbearable. I stare at the floor, waiting for him to say more.

"Why don't you go down to Belinda's in the morning and see if she wants to help you with your Mustang?"

I swallow, trying hard not to burst into tears in front of him. "Okay."

I'm not even sure she'll want to see me anymore, but I'm still excited about going to see her. Hopefully, she can find it in her heart to forgive me for being such an ass.

Dad goes to turn the key to start the engine but stops. "I know I've been little good to you, but I'd like to help you with your car also … if you'd like?"

I sit upright and look Dad in the eye, stunned by his sudden interest. "I'd like that."

There's a moment of tension. We hardly ever talk, but he seems to be making an effort to reach out to me.

There's been something on my mind for a while, and now seems to be the right time to broach it. "Do you remember Ramsi?" I ask.

He looks me in the eye, his mouth slowly opening and his face tightening before he nods.

"Did you stop me from going to the brickworks because of his death?"

He nods again. "I felt so guilty for his death. It was *my* brickworks, and I was ultimately responsible for everyone's safety. His death nearly destroyed me. I just couldn't …" He draws a deep breath. "I just couldn't see you at the brickworks anymore. I kept picturing that happening to you."

I nod, blinking away my tears. His words tell me he does care. I hope that this will bring us closer and I can finally have a normal dad, someone I can call "father." I think about Ramsi and what that must have been like for

Dad, not to mention that he has lost two wives. I'm starting to understand why he is the way he is; his soul has been forged in the fires of extreme pain and tragic loss. He's one of the toughest men I know to still be ticking after all that. I'm overwhelmed by a sense of empathy for him. I know I've been through a lot, but what he's been through … no one deserves to be dealt so much pain in one lifetime.

I feel a tear hanging from the corner of my eye and know it's about to race down my cheek, so I look out the side window so Dad can't see it.

He finally starts the engine and pulls out onto the road. My head is pounding and I'm so tired, all I want to do is go home and sleep for a month, but then again, knowing I'm allowed to see Belinda has me nervously anticipating our next meeting. I don't know whether she'll even talk to me, but I have to try.

Chapter 18

I wake in the morning after six hours of sleep, the best night's sleep I've had in months. I scoff down breakfast and head to Belinda's. It's only eight o'clock but I know that she and her parents will already be up.

As I walk down her driveway, I have second thoughts. I've been avoiding her all week, and she's no doubt pissed off and will probably tell me to go to hell, but I can't chicken out, I have to try.

Belinda opens the front door, her face strained with a mix of emotions when she sees me.

"Hey," I say softly.

"Hey," she replies with a hint of anger.

There's an awkward silence. She just stands there. Finally, she steps outside, closing the door behind her.

"I'm sorry for avoiding you at school," I say.

She shakes her head and sits on the front steps.

She seems receptive, so I sit next to her, but she frowns suddenly and looks me right in the eye. "Do you want to see one another or not?" she asks angrily with tears starting to form.

I glance away, feeling horrible about how I treated her. "I'm sorry for pushing you away."

Her face softens, and she gives me a sympathetic look. "What's going on with you?" she asks, trying to blink away her tears.

"I've been really struggling with Mom's death," I say, but I know it's not enough, I have to tell her everything, no matter how hard it is or how she might react. "I've had terrible depression and have been seeing a psychiatrist since Mom's death."

Her mouth pops open in surprise.

I swallow hard, trying with everything I have not to burst into tears myself. "It's a darkness I pray you'll never see. When I'm not wishing it was Dad that died in the accident instead of Mom, I'm wishing it was me."

Belinda cries. She looks completely lost for words. We sit quietly for a while.

"I've been getting better though, slowly. Dad said I could see you again."

Belinda jerks her head back and fixes her gaze on me. "What? What are you talking about?"

I suddenly realize I never told her about being banned from seeing her. "Oh ... my dad told me I couldn't see you ... he doesn't like your dad."

"What? Why?"

"He thinks your dad's lazy because he doesn't work ..." I say, trying to soften it as much as I can. "Plus, I kind of chewed his ear off because of the way he greeted your dad the other day."

"Did you tell him my dad *can't* work?"

I nod. "After he said I couldn't see you ... I did. I don't think he knew. He kinda looked surprised."

Belinda is still crying, and I reach out and hold her hand.

"I'm sorry. He's admitted that he was wrong and said that we can see each other again ... if you like."

I try to read her face. She wipes her eyes and avoids eye contact for a moment, like something is weighing on her mind.

"What's wrong?" I ask.

"That explosion in the news ... was that you?" She has concern written all over her face.

I look away, giving away my guilt.

"You need to be careful," she says softly. "There are people that care about you. *I* care about you."

"I'm sorry," I say, feeling stupid for doing something so dangerous.

"No ... *I'm* sorry," Belinda says. "I should have known something was wrong ... I should have come to check on you."

We sit quietly, lost in our thoughts.

"I'd still like to hang out ... if you do?" I ask after a while.

Belinda smiles, looking more light-hearted. "I'd like that."

Knowing she's back in my life warms my heart. "Dad asked if you want to help me with my Mustang."

Her face lights up. "Yeah! Of course ... I'd love to. Just a second and I'll get changed ... come in and say hello."

I wipe my eyes and face as I follow Belinda inside. Her father is in his usual chair. I step into the living room, give him a thin smile and a nervous wave.

"Kyle, nice to see you," he says, struggling to his feet. "What's left to do on your Mustang?"

"Just the inlet manifold and carburetor."

"Would you like a hand getting the engine back in? Getting the engine back in is a fair bit harder than pulling it out. I could ask a mechanic buddy of mine to help."

"Who's that? Charley?" Belinda asks, as she enters the room after getting changed into some old clothes. She must be excited about the two of us working on the car again; she got changed lightning fast.

Warren nods. "Yeah, he's always keen to help out on other people's cars."

"Yeah. That would be great," I say.

"Do you think you'll be ready to go tomorrow? I could get him to come around first thing in the morning if you like."

"What do you think?" I ask Belinda.

"Yeah, easily!"

"All right. And your father will be okay with us coming around?" Warren asks cautiously.

I feel horrible for the way both Dad and I have treated Warren and Belinda, so I try hard to give Warren a positive response. "Yeah, sure. He said he would help too."

"Sounds good, we'll see you around eight?"

"That would be great. Thank you."

"Don't mention it, buddy. We all want to see that Mustang back on the road."

I smile and swallow, my eyes tearing up a little.

Belinda joins me in the garage at the crack of dawn and we go to work finishing off the engine. She's so beautiful, and I love being around her so much, I can see why William says ties with the community are important. My mood has already lifted significantly.

As we're putting the finishing touches on the engine, we hear a really loud rumble coming down the driveway.

"What the hell is that?" I ask.

Belinda chuckles. "That's Charley's '68 Camaro."

When we step outside, I gawk at the car. It's in pristine condition, painted sky blue with lots of chrome. You can clearly see your reflection in its high-gloss paint.

Belinda smiles. "It has a 427 big block."

I smirk that Belinda would know that.

"That's one nice ride you've got there," I say to Charley.

"Yeah, you should see my credit card," he says. "It's going to be in the muscle car show in Denver in a couple of weeks."

"Oh yeah. I wouldn't mind going to that," I say, wondering if Belinda would like to go too. Then I think, well of course she would. I should ask her, and I could drive us in the Mustang. It would be a good way for us to spend more time with one another once the Mustang's finished too.

We've only just started working when Dad walks out. He's in his everyday jeans and a work shirt, and I'm not sure whether he's leaving to go to work or has come out to help. My stomach sinks as I wait for him to tell me that he'll be back in a couple of hours. But instead, he surprises me.

"All right, what can I help with?" he asks.

I'm relieved and feel a sense of happiness I haven't felt in a long time. Belinda and Warren stop what they're doing and look at him. After an awkward greeting, Charley pulls him over to show him how to replace the engine mounts.

I get back to work, trying to break the tension. Belinda and I are transferring the engine from the stand to the hoist. I look up at her from time to time, watching her work. Her face is happy. She has so much energy, and I'm thankful for how joyous she is to be around. I hope nothing else comes between us again.

Surprisingly, Charley and Dad seem to get along quite well, although I can see that Warren is still hesitant, only speaking to Dad when absolutely necessary. It's understandable. I can see Dad trying at least, and I guess that's all I can ask for. We may never be really close, but it would be good if we could be friends, to talk amicably at least.

The engine's in, the bonnet's back on, and we're cleaning up all the tools, which are spread all over the garage floor.

"Well, that's it, Kyle," Warren says. "How about you give it a kick in the guts and see if it will start?"

I have a huge grin on my face as I sit down in the driver's seat. It's been months since I've even sat in it. Everyone stands around watching in anticipation as I turn the key. It cranks over and over but doesn't fire.

Charley leans over the engine and tinkers with the carburetor. "Give it another go now."

I try again, and it roars to life. Without the air filter on, I can hear it sucking down copious amounts of air. There are smiles all round, and Belinda and Warren both clap and cheer. Dad's even smiling, for the first time in a long time. I tear up when I see the joy on his face.

"Want to take it for a spin?" I say to Belinda.

"Hell yeah!" she says, racing around to the passenger's side and jumps in.

Charley fits the air filter quickly and closes the bonnet. He gives me the thumbs up, and I reverse out of the garage.

When we make it to the top of the driveway, Belinda's cheeks are turning pink with glee. Mine are probably too. I pull out onto the road and push the throttle. It splutters a few times and then takes off. Belinda has the window down. It's a bit too chilly, but I don't mind, I'm just grateful for having her in my life. I look over at her gorgeous face, her hair flowing backward in the wind. She returns my smile and my heart warms.

After seeing it sit in the garage for so long, in pieces and not running, I had been starting to think I'd never see it on the road again. So, to see it finally done is pretty epic. It may be filled with rust and look pretty ragged, but I wouldn't swap it for the world. It's such an achievement, and I'm so glad that Belinda was here to help me with it. William was definitely right, us sharing something that matters to both of us has brought us closer, and through that bond, I feel like we have a future together.

As we approach the lookout, I decide to pull over and kill the engine. The closest thing to a date we've been on is when we went to the museum, which was more of a pseudo date. With my confidence building from completing the car and Belinda and I now getting on like it was before, I decide it's time I should ask her out officially.

I glance over at her, my newfound confidence waning slightly. "I was wondering ..." I say and trail off, my nerves getting the better of me.

Belinda looks at me blankly. "What?"

"Would you like to go on a date?"

She laughs and my heart sinks. I worry that she's going to say no but then pull myself together. I'm hoping her laugh is just because she's shocked that I asked so formally, after we've been hanging out for such a long time.

She covers her mouth briefly, apologizing for the laugh. "Sorry ... yeah, I'd love to."

I breathe a sigh of relief and she gives me a beaming smile.

"Where will we go?" she asks.

I shrug. "I know it's a cliché, but I was thinking of dinner and a movie, Friday night?"

"Yeah, that would be nice."

We're both grinning as I restart the engine.

I've been sleeping well lately, and I'm feeling refreshed, but my heart's racing as I get ready for our first official date. I look at myself in the bathroom mirror and am reminded of the horrible vision I had here, that time I was brushing my teeth. My body's filled with a mix of emotions: excitement, hope, love for Belinda, but also a vulnerability, like I'm standing on the edge of a tall building – like I could still fall back into despair and drowning depression at any moment.

Dad walks in and looks me up and down with a smile. Our eyes meet. There's something different about him lately – more than him helping me with the car or opening up about Ramsi. There's something he's not telling me, I'm sure of it. Without saying anything, he walks away with a curious smile. *Weirdo.* I scoff, but with a smile.

I put on Mom's necklace, feeling the gold feather between my fingers. I wonder if I should have bought Belinda some flowers, then think again; she'd probably laugh herself silly if I turned up at hers with a bouquet.

When I pull up in front of her house, someone is peering through the blinds. My heart's racing, which is crazy; it's not like we haven't done anything together before.

I knock on the front door.

Belinda's mom answers. "Hi Mrs. Andrews, how are you?"

"Hi, Kyle, I'm well, thanks. Belinda's just finishing getting ready. Come on in."

No sooner do I get inside, Belinda comes out. She's actually wearing a dress. It's light blue with a few large red flowers here and there and stops several inches short of her knees. Maybe I should have bought flowers. My heart speeds as she smiles at me.

"Hey," she says, blushing.

I return her smile.

Her mom's grinning hard and even looks like she has tears in her eyes. I can see Warren behind her, shuffling out to see us off.

After the movie, we're walking back to my car when Belinda reaches over and takes my hand. I glance over to find her smiling to herself. I love how she can be just as happy elbows deep in grease and car parts, but at the same time feel comfortable getting dressed up. She turns heads in the slim-fitting dress and short heels, which makes me even more excited about holding hands and where this date could go.

Logan's car is parked a couple of spots up from my car, and Joseph and Logan are leaning against the trunk, smoking. They're both leering at Belinda, making me want to smash the two numbskulls' heads together.

"Did you really rebuild your Mustang's engine?" Joseph asks.

Logan is throwing daggers with his eyes. Belinda looks at me.

"Yeah," I reply emphatically as I unlock the passenger's side door.

Joseph laughs loudly and digs Logan in the ribs. "You gotta give 'im a drag race!"

Logan scowls. "My car would flog that rust bucket!"

"Want a bet?" Belinda says before sliding into her seat.

I close her door and walk around to the driver's side, smiling to myself.

As I climb in, I steal a rare peek at her legs. I can't help but picture making love to her. I've never had sex before, and I hold the idea in great anticipation. I can imagine sharing that experience with Belinda – my soulmate – would be unforgettable.

"What," she asks in a soft voice.

My heart skips a beat. "Oh … nothing."

She smiles, but her eyebrows turn down in a slight frown.

We leave the city and head home. Not wanting the night to end, I decide to drive through Boulder, instead of taking the bypass. It's after eleven o'clock, and other than the few pubs and takeaway shops that are still open, the place is a ghost town.

Something catches my eye in the rear-view mirror as I pull up at a set of traffic lights near the outskirt of town. I don't have time to register what I saw, before a car – just seconds later – comes tearing to a halt alongside us. A figure lowers the window, and I see it is Logan. Joseph is riding shotgun.

My heart races.

"Do you need a push?" Logan yells at the top of his lungs.

Belinda gives them the finger before turning to me and saying, "Kick his ass!"

Logan's turbocharged four-cylinder is whizzing as he pumps the throttle. My engine's barely run in, but stuff it. I hit the throttle too, and the roar drowns out everything.

The lights go green and we both floor it. Logan gets a jump start as my tires spin, but I manage to get in front. We pass forty miles an hour and tear out of town.

With my foot pressed to the gas, I watch as the speedometer increases. I know what lies ahead: a tee-intersection with a barbed wire fence right in front, skirting a grassy field. With adrenaline raging through my veins, I remember stealing Dad's gun and the bomb. I'm thrilled to be playing with death once more as all rational thought leaves my mind, and I have to remind myself that Belinda is with me. Having only spent money on the engine and nothing at all on the brakes, I'm nervous of how the car will react, so when we hit one hundred miles an hour, I ease up. We approach the tee-junction and I slam on the brakes. Belinda's holding on tight as we're both slammed forward into our seatbelts.

A moment later, Logan goes whizzing past.

I'm braking with everything I have and am barely going to stop in time.

Logan isn't so lucky, and he skids straight through the intersection, crashing through the fence and into the grassy field. His car rolls over and over in a dizzying flash of lights, parts flying into the air. When he finally comes to rest, steam is pouring from the radiator, the roof is all mangled, and several windows are smashed.

Belinda and I get out, opened mouthed. *Should we help? Are they okay?*

A few seconds pass before one of the doors opens and Joseph crawls out.

Sirens wail from behind us. I look over at Belinda, unsure what to do.

"He's getting out," Belinda says, her voice shaky.

I look back to the mangled car and see Logan climbing out and collapsing on the grass. I can just make out blood running down his face, but it looks like he'll live. I follow Belinda's stare back toward town – a police car is heading in our direction at great speed.

"They'll be okay. We need to get the hell out of here," Belinda says, before jumping back in.

I drop back into my seat, slam my door and floor it. As I drive out of town, Belinda looks out the rear window. I'm constantly glancing up at the rear-view mirror, afraid of whether we have been seen. My heart is pounding in my chest at the chaos of what just happened. "Do you think they'll be okay?"

Belinda nods. "I think so. They got out all right."

On the way home, my heart rate stays elevated, and I can't clear my mind. I can't believe I just did that. That was really stupid. I'd never forgive myself if Belinda got hurt from my careless driving. The more I think about it, the more furious I am with myself for being baited by Logan.

It's almost as if Belinda can tell that I need some time to calm down, as she says, "Would you like to go to the lookout before taking me home?"

I appreciate her trying to lighten the mood. I look her in the eyes in the minimal light and nod.

The view from the lookout is spectacular at night. It's approaching midnight, and Boulder can be seen at the foot of the mountains, with the Denver city lights sparkling in the distance. There's no one else here.

Belinda places her hand on my leg. "What's wrong?" she asks.

I shake my head, still mad at myself. "That was stupid."

"It was just a bit of fun ... dangerous in hindsight, but fun," she says light-heartedly.

I turn on the interior light so I can see her and give her a serious look. "I've been discussing my dangerous behavior with William. He says it's common for people that are suffering from depression to become increasingly self-destructive, the more depressed they get."

"Don't beat yourself up. We're all okay."

"Normally I would agree, but after the copper bombs, the cannon, and then the really big bomb, I tend to agree with him. I can't keep going like this."

Belinda rubs my hand with her thumb. "You've been feeling better now though, haven't you?"

I nod. "Yeah ... I have to stop doing all these crazy things though. I ..."

Belinda looks at me, waiting for me to finish talking. "What?"

My heart races. "I love you ..." I say. "And I don't want to see anything happen to you."

Belinda's mouth curves into a smile. "I love you too."

I feel the warmth in my chest as she reciprocates. I can't believe I just said that. I can't believe *she* just said that.

She kisses me on the cheek. "You watch ... things will return to normal soon."

After expressing our love for one another, I feel like I can tell her anything. I think about my time in Egypt and losing Ramsi, and I wonder if it's something I should share with her. It might help her understand my depression and my past, but it might also push her away.

"What's on your mind?" she asks.

"Can I tell you something?"

She gives me an intense look and a nod.

"When we were in Egypt, I had a friend, Ramsi. I was only eleven when we moved there, and I really struggled to make friends. When I was thirteen, I started working at Dad's brickworks and made friends with one of the local kids, Ramsi. We started playing after school on the days we didn't work at the brickworks. He was a funny kid, always laughing at my Arabic and just generally making fun of things. One day ... Ramsi was crushed in the brick press and killed."

Belinda gasps. "Oh my god. Did you see it?"

I nod, blinking away tears.

Belinda shakes her head in shock.

"After losing Mom, I've had a lot of trouble getting close to people. I've been burdened by this feeling, that if I get close to someone, they'll die," I admit.

Belinda is frowning, clearly deep in thought for a moment before replying. "You've been through so much. You don't have to worry about me though ... I'm not going anywhere," she says, giving me a reassuring smile. Then she leans over, using my shoulder as a pillow.

I rest my cheek against the top of her head and feel her warmth.

The memory of Ramsi has been buried for so long, now being able to talk about it has made me feel like I can move on with my life. I know my own mood has definitely lifted, and I feel like there's a change in the air. Telling William about my delusions has lifted an enormous weight from my shoulders, and having Belinda to talk to about my feelings and my past has made me feel almost human again.

I've prayed that what they say is true, that it's always darkest before dawn. I hope that after everything I've been through, tomorrow will be the start of a new chapter in my life.

The next morning, when I sit up in bed, I'm surprised to see the time. Nine o'clock! That's the best I've slept in a long time. I turn down my sheet and swing my feet to the floor, smiling to myself, remembering how Belinda had said she loves me.

Dad's in the kitchen when I walk in.

"How was the date?" he asks.

"Good," I say non-committedly. Things have improved between us lately, but I still struggle to open up to him.

"You got a minute?" he asks, his face deadpan.

Crap! I hope he hasn't found out about the drag race last night.

"Yeah," I reply hesitantly.

We sit at the dining table, and he looks me in the eye, swallowing as if he's about to spit out some big news. "I've sold my majority share in the company. I no longer work at the brickworks."

I gasp, my eyes widening. "What? Why?" I thought they'd be carrying him out of that place in a pine box.

"So I can spend more time with you. My heart just wasn't in it anymore."

My heart, on the other hand, sinks.

Although I've been craving for a normal dad, one I can do things with, I now feel guilty. "But that's been your life's work."

"Yeah, but I want to start a new life – and plus, you need me. Neither of us could keep going like that."

"What will you do?" I ask, feeling concerned for him.

He shakes his head. "I don't know, but I thought as a start ... that I'd take you to that muscle car show in Denver."

I'm shocked. That's the first time he's instigated doing something with me in years. I've already asked

Belinda, but I nod anyway. Hopefully, he won't mind if she comes too.

I sit for a moment, taking in all he has said. "What made you decide to sell your share?"

Dad mashes his bottom lip into his top lip. "I haven't been happy there for a long time. I was just going through the motions each day, not challenged or learning anything new. I enjoyed the first few years in Egypt, but then when ...Well, you know. And after the past few weeks, seeing you suffering, I decided it's more important for me to be here for you, and I've only got you here for another year or so, at which point I guess you'll leave and head on out into the world to start your own life ..." He's rambling. I guess he must feel nervous to be saying all this to me, after all this time.

All I can do is nod, as I'm getting too choked up to speak. I'm close to tears after everything that's happened. Although I'm ecstatic to hear he wants to spend time with me, I can't escape feeling riddled with guilt.

Chapter 19

The Mesektet must be nearing the eastern akhet, as light fills the sky like no other hour of the night. My heart glows, for the majesty of Ra being reborn as Khepri is close at hand.

As Anput and I accompany Aya, Eman, and Shani toward the Field of Reeds on foot, we can hear a ceaseless roar. Red and orange light flickers in the sky. To the north, Tau is meandering through the desert. He's escaped the clutches of Sokar and an afterlife of servitude in the army of the damned, has failed in judgement, and after being swallowed by the serpentine shadowy floor of the Hall of the Two Truths, has been spat out into the desert.

"O Lord Anubis, what will become of Tau?" Shani asks.

"The Osiris Shani, as Horus is a defender of Osiris, he will see Tau to his destiny. While he wasn't caught with the stolen hearts, clay, or pages from the Book of Thoth, I believe in my heart it was he who stole. For he was a thief in the mundane world."

Before long, the Island of Fire comes into view. The rectangular pool of fire flickers and roars. On each side, there is a brazier. On each corner, there is a baboon, which sits and stares toward the akhets. When Tau sees the island, he runs, for like the waters of Nun, the Island of Fire is where evildoers are cast to die a second death.

A high-pitched screech sounds from above.

We stop dead in our tracks and look to the sky.

Horus, in the form of a falcon, is circling overhead. His feathers flutter as he eyes Tau from high above. Tau runs as fast as he can, tripping and staggering as he glances over his shoulder. Horus folds his wings in and dives, his feathers ruffling as he plummets. With his wings flared, talons outstretched, he slows and homes in on his target. As he drives his sharp talons into Tau's shoulders, Tau screams. Horus lifts Tau off the ground, thudding the air with his wings, over and over. Tau's harrowing screams echo over the land.

Horus releases Tau, and he falls. Legs and arms flailing, he cries out in vain. When he lands upon the island, he bursts into flames, and in seconds Tau is nay more. His corrupt life on Earth, his heavy heart, has finally caught up with him – and now, he ceases to exist.

With the Island of Fire behind us, and as we near the Field of Reeds, the surrounding landscape changes dramatically. We are seeing vegetation once again and before too long, vast fields of lush wheat and barley.

"O Lord Anubis, have we made it to the Field of Reeds? Are they up ahead?"

"Indeed."

Shani's face glows with joy.

We stop at the shore of a system of rivers and alcoves, all connected by mesmerizing blue water. The ba of many work the land, reaping with sickles, sitting before mounds of wheat and barley. The ba of people and oxen plow the fields. Others row upon the waters in barks, while some worship the gods.

The sky suddenly brightens like dawn in the mundane world. Light beams down upon the Field of Reeds, and its warmth caresses our faces.

Shani drops to her knees and raises her palms. "*Al hamdu Li Khepri, Ya ilahu al-Mashreq Al-Azeem.*"

Praise to Khepri, O Great God of the east.

A short while later, she stands. "O Lord Anubis, how long will we be blessed by the sunlight of Khepri?"

"For this hour of the night," I say. "It is time to live as you did on Earth."

"O Lord Anubis, but I am a scholar like Thoth. I do not know how to plow a field or reap with a sickle. I was buried with a timber shabti, carved in my image. Can it do work for me?"

I bow toward Shani in acknowledgment and then follow her stare.

Anput reaches into her pocket and pulls out Shani's timber shabti. "The Osiris Shani," Anput says, holding her palm out with the shabti standing upright, "your shabti will do work for thou, if the words thou know."

Shani speaks a spell from the Book of the Dead to bring her shabti to life: "O shabti of mine, may your members hail, may you go forth into the fields, may you go forth and do work for me in my stead. I am in the sacred place with the Gods of Embalming. Go forth O shabti of mine."

Just as Shani finishes reciting her spell, Anput withdraws her hand and the shabti hovers in thin air. A dozen pinpoints of white light start buzzing around the shabti in a random dance, leaving short streaks of white

305

light in their trail. The pinpoints of light speed faster and faster before flying into the chest of the shabti. The shabti grows larger and larger to the sound of timber creaking. Once it's full size and its feet are standing upon the ground, it takes a deep breath, its first breath. Now at full size, the shabti looks identical to Shani in every way.

Shani takes a step back in astonishment, as do Aya and Eman.

Shani's shabti holds her sickle to one side and bows, before looking Shani in the eye. "The Osiris Shani, I will do work in the Field of Reeds, in your name, and the honor shall be mine."

"O shabti of mine, thank you," Shani says with a bow.

Aya and Eman lead Shani's shabti, leave us and head toward a group of farmers who are plowing fields, their faces joyous as they're reunited with their friends.

I take Shani's hand and we approach the northern waterway where Ani the scribe is rowing upon the waters in a bark.

Shani's face lights up. "O Lord Anubis, Anput, can we take a ride in a bark?"

My heart glows for the ba of Shani's own warmth. "Indeed."

I signal Ani, and he makes his way over to us. Ripples fan out from the stern as he pulls the oar in and out of the calm water. As the keel rides up on the sandy shore, he draws the oar aboard.

"O Ani, can we ride in your bark," Shani asks.

Ani is wearing a kilt made of flax and stands in the prow. "O certainly. Your blessed soul and the gods of the necropolis are most welcome." He holds his hand out for Shani to take.

She steps into the bark and takes a seat.

"O Lord Anubis, Anput, I am humbled by your company," Ani says as we join him. He pushes off and begins to row.

Anput takes my hand. Sitting alongside my soulmate for eternity, after shepherding another blessed soul through the Kingdom of Osiris, brings me such joy. I can imagine what it must be like for Khepri to light up the sky at dawn. It must be incredible for your ba to burst into flames, to shine light upon the Earth and give life to so many.

Shani sits alongside Ani, in silent joy and contemplation. Ani strokes the oar through the water, creating the soothing sound of trickling water, as the timber oar clunks gently against the timber gunwale. Out on the water, there are alcoves filled with green reeds where fowl swim, their legs paddling speedily below the surface of the clear water. The sound of the reeds rustling in the soft breeze is calming, and with sunlight upon my face, I feel at peace.

Chapter 20

It's Saturday morning, and on the way in to see William, Belinda and I stop by the cemetery. Belinda gives me a sympathetic face when we arrive, and I kill the engine.

Belinda takes my hand as we walk toward Mom's grave.

The cemetery looks so different now – green, with flowers blooming in a rainbow of colors. In the distance, groundskeepers are picking up fallen leaves and branches, and we can see and hear a chorus of birds fluttering from tree to tree, chirping. It's only morning, but it's already quite warm. I stop and take my jumper off, and Belinda immediately retakes my hand.

"I wish I met your mom."

I give her a thin smile. "She would have liked you … and you her."

Mom's tombstone comes into view. I remember how I had broken into tears at William's when I was hit by the realization that I'd never see her again, but I wonder if today will be the day I'll see her go-forth-by-day. I try to shake the thought.

We stand in front of her grave. Belinda shakes her head ever so slightly.

"What?" I ask.

"She was only thirty-eight," she says, her voice full of melancholy.

"My birth mom was only twenty-five."

Belinda's face softens, and she gives me a hug. When she lets go, she wipes a tear away and we both sit on the grass.

It's a stellar day, and I try to think of all the good things in my life instead of focusing on the imperfections. I do after all have Belinda in my life, and we've grown so close now. I still can't quite believe that she said she loves me. And now that Dad's sold his stake in his company, our relationship might even improve.

Belinda sits quietly. I admire her beautiful face and luscious wavy brown hair.

The loud chirps of a large bird catch my attention. A golden eagle soars overhead, sliding across the sky, its golden-brown feathers ruffling in the rising warm air. My heart skips a beat, for somehow, in my heart, I know it's Mom's ba. It's something I've dreamed of for so long, to see her again on Earth. The bird spirals downwards, and when it's just a few feet off the ground, she transforms from an eagle into her human form, wearing a long white dress, and she touches down gracefully before walking toward us.

I wonder how much of the experience is just my mind's eye and how much of it is real. Mom's semitranslucent body leads me to believe she is here in a purely incorporeal sense.

She sits beside Belinda on the grass. Her golden Egyptian complexion and cascading dark hair give her such a striking appearance. I picture her shabti doing work for her in the Field of Reeds while she visits us here on Earth. Mom glances over at Belinda and then gives me a big smile. Her smile melts my heart.

I too glance over at Belinda, who seems to be smiling at Mom. When I look back, Mom's ba is fading, becoming more and more translucent until she vanishes completely.

I feel a little sad it was such a fleeting moment, but I feel warmth for having gotten to see her on Earth once more.

We sit for a while longer, taking in the tranquility and the growing heat of the late spring morning. "It feels like it could be a warm one today."

Belinda nods.

"We should get going … don't want to be late," I say.

Belinda rises to her feet and helps me up. Without thinking, I reach out and touch Mom's tombstone. Feeling the course stone beneath my fingertips, I was expecting to see a vision of the Duat, but nothing happens, and I'm a little relieved.

As we drive into the city, I glance over at Belinda. "What are you going to do while I'm at William's?"

"I thought I'd do some window-shopping. You'll only be an hour, won't you?"

I nod. As I pull up in the front of William's office, I remember the last time I was here, how I left feeling completely eviscerated. I can't believe how much things have turned around since then.

I lean over and kiss Belinda on the cheek. "See you in a bit."

When I enter the reception, William does a double take.

"You look better," he says.

I smile. "Yeah, feeling a lot better."

"That's great," he says as I follow him into the back room.

"So, what's been happening?" he asks as we sit down.

"Where do I start? I finished my Mustang, Belinda and I went on an official date, and Dad sold his share in his company ... he even helped put the engine back in my car!"

William sits wide-eyed and smiling. "That's amazing. I'm really glad to hear that. And how has the new medication been?"

"I've been feeling a lot better. The antidepressants have helped my mood. I wouldn't say they are solely responsible, but they played a part. I know I still have work to do, to deepen my ties with the community, but even knowing people, Belinda, her parents and others, has made me feel more a part of the community and not such an outcast."

"How have your delusions been going?" he asks.

I recall seeing Mom at the cemetery this morning but refrain from telling him about it. "They're easing ... they don't seem to be as vivid, and they don't seem to last as long either."

"That's good to hear. Do you think you've gained closure?"

I nod. "Yeah, I think so. Belinda and I visited Mom's grave this morning."

William is clearly pleased to hear me say this, but not long after I finish speaking, he suddenly frowns, as if he snagged some random thought that was floating around in the back of his mind. "What's your dad going to do now?"

I shrug. "I don't know … I felt so guilty when he told me what he had done."

"Why is that?"

"I felt selfish. That he sold his life's work just for me."

"Do you remember when I said that you should also show yourself compassion?"

I nod and smile. The thought was once so alien, but now I'm able to cut myself a break and stop feeling so guilty about Dad's decision.

"And your plans on what you want to do after school, have you made any progress here?"

"Yeah. I'm going to try to knuckle down next year to lift my grades. I've been thinking about maybe going back to Egypt for a year, but … I'm a bit worried that in doing so, I'll cut all my ties with the community and end up back at square one."

"Yeah, that is a concern," William says. "Moving around a lot can be difficult. If you go, you'll have to put in extra effort when you get there to establish new ties.

And has having a plan for the future helped with your mood?"

"Yeah. It's given me something to look forward to."

"Well, don't forget everything we've spoken about. Keep your intrinsic values and steer away from extrinsic ones, don't settle with having just one friend, continue to put effort into maintaining and making new friends. If you go to Egypt, once you reach that long-term goal, make sure to come up with a new one. It's important to always have something to look forward to," he says, smiling. "Isn't it funny how life can turn on a dime?"

I return his smile. I never thought I'd put the darkness behind me, but now, four months after the accident, I finally feel like I can begin to move on with my life.

When I step outside, Belinda is sitting in the car. She gives me a smile as I cross the road. I feel a sense of genuine happiness when I hop in and start the engine. It's the first time I've felt that in a long time.

"William was watching you cross the road," Belinda says. "He was standing in the doorway, grinning to himself."

I chuckle. I can't imagine what it must be like to help someone so stricken with grief and depression. I won't ever forget William and what he's done for me, for us.

When we arrive back at home, I see Dad's truck is parked outside and both roller doors are up. I park in my side of the garage and gawk at the scene: benches, cupboard doors, and a sink are littering Dad's side.

"What the hell?" I say, taking in the scene around me.

"Is your dad putting in a new kitchen?"

I shrug. "Must be."

When we enter the kitchen, Dad's breaking the old kitchen apart with a sledgehammer. He jumps when he sees us.

He smiles. "Oh ... Hi, Belinda."

Belinda waves. "Hi, Mr. Roberts."

"What are you doing?" I ask.

"I was bored, so I thought I'd put a new kitchen in," he says, still smiling.

Belinda and I both chuckle and head to my room.

"Your dad's so different now ... do you think he was suffering from depression too?"

"I don't know; he never talks about his feelings. I'd be surprised if he wasn't, though."

We sit on the end of my bed, bored. Now that my Mustang's finished, there's nothing to do, although ... it's warm out.

"Do you want to go for a swim down at the lake?" I ask.

Belinda smiles. "Aw ... yeah, that'd be nice."

I grab my board shorts and a beach towel and head to the bathroom to get changed. I've been looking forward to going swimming with Belinda for weeks. It's normally hidden under layers of clothes, but I know she's got a rocking body under there.

Belinda unlocks her front door, and we make our way inside. All the blinds are closed, and it's noticeably cooler in here than the warm air outside. I sit on one of the lounges and wait for Belinda to get changed. Her folks are gone, and it's peacefully quiet – not that her house is usually rowdy. I look at Warren's chair and wonder if Dad will ever be like him. It's unlikely, but maybe we can find some middle ground. Him helping on my car was such a refreshing change of pace.

Belinda reemerges a short while later. "You ready?"

I do a double take as I jump up. She's wearing a conventional light blue, short denim skirt with frayed edges, a white lacy embroidery top that's semi-see through, and a black bikini beneath.

Belinda frowns slightly. "What?"

"Nothing." I look her in the eye and joke, "I didn't know you owned normal clothes."

She punches me hard on the shoulder, and I head to the front door grinning.

We walk through the woods toward the lake. It's only ten o'clock, but it's already quite hot. There's something about a crystal-clear sky and the warmth from the sun's rays that makes you feel alive. I smile to myself, feeling so much better than I did just a month ago. The snow and sub-freezing temperatures, I guess, also contributed to my depression. I follow Belinda to the shoreline and join her by her side. She looks at me, smiling, and holds my hand.

A short while later, we reach a sandy alcove and drop our gear. Belinda pulls her top up over her head and my heart races. She has a toned athletic body. *Damn.* I look away when she unzips her skirt. I don't know where she gets such a toned body from, she's not the sporty type, but then again, she's not a couch and movies type either – she's always doing something. I throw my shirt on the ground and enter the water. The enticing clear water sparkles as the ripples fan out across the surface.

Belinda tiptoes in. "It's cold."

I backstroke away from the shore. "It's okay once you're in."

When Belinda is waist deep, she finally lowers herself into the water and breaststrokes toward me. Her long brown hair is slicked back, and as she nears, she puts her hands on my shoulders and wraps her legs around my waist. She kisses me and I run my hands down her back. My heart's going a million miles an hour. She leans back with her arms outstretched and her face pointing skyward. Her eyes are closed as she takes in the sun's warmth.

I can't believe the way she makes me feel. I wish I could spend the rest of my life with her. Belinda swims around amusing herself for a short while before eyeing me with a knowing look.

My heart skips a beat. I'd love to know what's going on inside her head right now. Like me, I don't think she's ever had sex before, but I'm sure it's something she thinks about. It would be perfect for us, as soulmates, to share that first experience with each other.

After we're all swum out, I follow Belinda to the shore. We both lie facedown on our beach towels as we dry in the heat. Belinda's skin is peppered with crystal-clear droplets of water that glisten in the sunlight. She cracks open her eyelids, and we both look into each other's eyes without so much as saying a word. With heat on my back and warmth in my heart, I feel like winter has finally broken.

After dinner, we sit in my car at the lookout and watch as the city lights sparkle like stars. The moonlight illuminates Belinda's face, accentuating her fair skin. She takes my hand, leans toward me and kisses me on the lips.

"When we finish school, would you like to go to Egypt with me?" I ask.

Her eyes widen in the dim light. "Yeah ... I'd love to."

Her sultry voice sets my heart on fire. The hot spring air casually breezes through the open windows, and Belinda kisses me again before climbing into the back seat.

I follow, and as she begins to unbutton the top of her shirt, I lean over her to kiss her. The heat between us is intense. Her ba is so alluring, so passionate, and her ka so full of life. I take her hand and we interweave our fingers. I haven't done this before, and I hope I'm doing it right. The way she exhales from the way I kiss her neck is a good sign. The smell of her hair feels like it's passing right through my body and being soaked up by my soul. I've never felt at greater peace than in the arms of my soulmate, my soulmate for eternity.

Belinda sits on my lap and leans forward, kissing me ever so softly. Every sense is acute – the feel of her soft skin, the sound of her breath, and the heat emanating from her body. As we kiss, we take off pieces of clothing, one by one, until it's just us.

My heart thumps deep like a drum in the Underworld.

Afterward, we're both sprinkled in fine droplets of perspiration. I run the tips of my fingers over her skin and feel the moister coalesce beneath them. Belinda lies down and looks into my eyes. I kiss her again. The heat between us makes me feel like I'm about to burst into flames, like our bas and kas will be forged together in the intense heat and ascend to the celestial sphere as a unified akh to become the brightest star in the night sky.

The spring air finally cools, and I pull Belinda in close to stay warm. She uses my chest as a pillow, and I'm overwhelmed with a feeling of love and contentment. I never want this moment to end.

"Did you mean it when you asked if I wanted to go to Egypt with you?" she asks softly without moving.

I look down at the top of her head. "Yeah, of course ... I thought we could get an apartment in Cairo ... go see the pyramids together."

I feel her mouth curve into a smile against my chest.

"That'd be nice," she says sleepily.

It's so far away from our life out here; it's hard to picture being back in Egypt. But I can imagine showing Belinda around and her taking it all in with wide eyes and enthusiasm.

As I arrive home from school, I'm getting excited with just a few weeks until the summer break. Everything seems to be improving in leaps and bounds. My father has smiled more in the past week than he has in the past year. And after we went to the muscle car show with Belinda, the tension that was keeping us apart feels like it has been dissolving, and that we may have a somewhat normal relationship.

When I park in the garage, the new kitchen benches are nowhere to be seen, and as I enter the kitchen, I'm left breathless. The dark timber cupboards and white benchtop look amazing.

"Oh wow. Have you finished?" I ask, checking out his handiwork.

"Yeah, just gotta hook up the sink."

I give my father a smile as he walks over to the dining table. He pulls out a folded piece of paper from his wallet and hands it to me. It's a check. *What the hell?*

"I thought you could use it to have your Mustang resprayed like the one we saw in the car show," my father says.

I look him in the eyes. "Thank you ... but ... I don't want a paint job like that," I say, trying hard not to sound ungrateful.

"Why don't you get it resprayed to its original paint scheme then? After all the work and money you've put into rebuilding the engine, it would be a shame to just let the car crumble away from all the rust."

It's not a bad idea.

"Yeah ... okay," I reply.

I turn to face the kitchen and recall the memory of Mom standing on tiptoes to kiss me. With the new kitchen, it seems like that memory is harder to recall, which makes me a little sad. There's something I've always wanted to know, and now that we are finally talking to each other, I pluck up the courage to ask. "Do you think Mom will become an akh?"

My father's smile swells. "I'd like to think so ... I'd like to think that we all will one day, and we'll join her in the night sky."

My heart warms, and I return his smile. I'm guessing it's something they would have talked about. It's nice that Mom had such a positive influence on the both of us. Maybe that influence will be something that helps us bond. Something that we joyfully reminisce about some day.

Chapter 21

Anput and I walk by Shani's side as we take in the beauty of the Field of Reeds. It is truly majestic. The sunlight provided by Khepri is fading fast – a sign that he will soon make his way toward the Gap of Bakhu and leave the Duat for this night.

"O Lord Anubis, when Khepri leaves the Duat, what will happen to the people?"

"The Osiris Shani, they will sleep." I can see that something weighs heavy on Shani's mind. "The Osiris Shani, speak from your heart."

"I wish ... I wish to become an akh and join the gods in the celestial sphere."

I stop walking and turn to face her. "Only the purest of heart can ascend to the celestial sphere as an akh. Privilege to journey with Ra's entourage has been granted to you, for I know you, and I know your heart. It has always been your destiny to join the gods in the celestial sphere. It is only you who stood in the way. Released your burden you have, and now it is time, if you so wish, to join Khepri on his day-bark and ascend to the celestial sphere."

A great smile grows upon Shani's lips. "O Lord Anubis, I am ready."

Anput and I take her hands and we leave the Field of Reeds.

Walking through more desert, we spot the great lion of the east, Tomorrow. He trots toward us with his eyes fixed upon us and his tail swishing. As he nears, his great frame towers above us before he lies on the sand. His brown mane ruffles against the ground, and his yellow-brown eyes stare down at us, unblinking.

"The Osiris Shani," Tomorrow says, "thank you for being in Ra's entourage. As it has been for millions of years, and as it will be for millions more, it takes many for Ra to smite his demons. A matter a million times true."

Shani bows and turns her head up at the great lion. "O Tomorrow, I am honored to have been in Ra's entourage and I am pleased to have met you."

Tomorrow stands and looks upon us before leaving.

We head toward the great river where Horus is standing upon the shore. Now fully rejuvenated, Khepri stands upon the deck of his day-bark, the Mandjet, at the head of the gangplank awaiting our arrival. In this form, he has the head of a scarab beetle, wears a kilt with a bull's tail, and carries a was scepter and ankh.

Shani draws a deep breath. "O Khepri, I have been in your entourage and helped clear your path; I have assisted Isis; I have passed my judgement, and passage to my ka has been granted. May I join you on your day-bark?"

Khepri holds out his hand. "The Osiris Shani, you are welcome on my bark. You have helped ferry me from west to east, and now it is time for both of us to ascend."

Shani looks up at me with tears in her eyes. "O Lord Anubis, you are indeed a friend to the dead. I thank you and Anput, and I hope that someday we may meet again."

Anput and I smile at Shani.

She turns and boards the Mandjet. Horus pulls the gangplank ashore, and we watch as they make their way to the Gap of Bakhu.

And just like that, she's gone.

My heart is flooded with joy, for she has reached the most desired goal of many.

Horus turns to face us. "Anubis, Anput, I have received word from the Great Bennu Bird. Osiris wishes to speak with you in the Hall of the Two Truths."

I bow toward Horus – and together, we all journey westward.

When we enter the Hall of the Two Truths, it is empty except for two falcon-headed guards who stand at the entrance. I search Osiris' audience chamber, but naught do I find.

"For what purpose could transforming into Aya and Eman have?" I ask Anput, still unable to fathom the reason.

"Anubis, I do not know, it seems unlikely that someone would go to such lengths, and risk Osiris' wrath, to simply enter the Field of Reeds," Anput says, "but I feel Osiris might know, and that that is why we have been summoned."

I recall Heh's questions: for what purpose and why. "Why Aya and Eman?" I ask aloud.

"That is the question," Horus says.

"Nephthys told us about Tau; do you think she knows something?" I ask.

Anput takes my hand. "Anubis, your birth mother knew of Tau, and I believe it is likely Aya and Eman were targeted because of Tau's entry into the Duat of this night, but I cannot see Nephthys having anything to do with it, for why would she tell us of Tau in the first place?"

I shake my head. "I do not know."

Voices catch our attention. Aya and Eman are at the entrance, but the two guards have stopped them from entering. I signal to the guards to allow them in.

"Aya, Eman, what brings you here?" I ask.

Aya and Eman stand before Osiris' great throne. "Anubis," Aya says, teary eyed, "I wished to speak with you."

There is something that seems awry in her words, yet something so familiar. That is when I remember all that has come to pass, and I must question: which Aya and Eman stand before us? I peer into their chests and find that they have their hearts from Earth – the stolen hearts. It's the duplicate Aya and Eman!

"What is the meaning of this? Reveal yourselves immediately," I yell, but as I'm saying the words, I look deep into their hearts and find two dark souls. One so filled with deceit and villainy it can only be one person. The truth in their hearts cannot escape me. The souls standing before us stole the clay from the Lake of Natron and the pages from the Book of Thoth, and they forced Tau to steal the hearts for them.

"Who is it?" Horus and Anput ask in unison.

"Seth and Nephthys!" I say, taking a step back.

"Anubis, forgive me," Nephthys says. "But my place is by my husband's side. I asked to meet you here so I could say goodbye."

"You can tell your father that naught can stop us now," Seth says, pointing his finger at me.

Seth and Nephthys take each other's hands and run toward the gold double-leaf doors at the foot of Osiris' throne – the portal to the necropolis on Earth. The doors are normally impenetrable, but when Seth and Nephthys reach them, they pass right through, disappearing.

Anput and I stand opened mouthed, while Horus approaches the doors and pushes on them, but they don't budge.

I pace back and forth, furious. "I can't believe how nefarious my birth mother has become. I blame Seth, for his heavy heart is corrupt and putrid."

Anput takes my hand to stop me. "Anubis, be calm, for your father will know what to do."

"Where is he anyway?" Horus says. "Guard, find Osiris at once!"

"How could she do this?" I ask.

Anput looks into my eyes. She says naught, but the mere presence of her soul calms my fury.

Osiris and Isis enter, and I'm at odds on how to tell them. Osiris sits in his throne and Isis stands by his side. As I fill them in, they both open their mouth slightly, in shock.

"They mean to rejoin their kas in the necropolis. If successful, immortals they will becometh," Osiris says. "They mean to rule over Egypt."

"Anubis," Isis says, "they must have stolen more than just transformative spells from the Book of Thoth to be able to pass through the golden doors."

"Indeed," I say, feeling completely gutted with betrayal.

"Anubis, Anput, stopped they must be. Lest they be allowed to rule over Egypt. You must stop them and return Aya's and Eman's hearts."

Anput and I look up at Osiris in surprise.

I glance over at Anput before looking my father in the eye. "Osiris, we would be honored to carry out your will."

"Transform into that which your souls desire," Osiris says. "Leave the Duat through the golden doors, rejoin your kas on Earth, becometh immortals you will. You will journey far and wide, take on many forms, and traverse the expanse of time to see to my will."

Anput and I have spent countless years by each other's side and immediately know what the other is thinking. We both feel honor and joy to be returning to Earth.

Together, Anput and I say, "Osiris, we would be honored to return to Earth, to be charged with your will."

Anput and I face each other and simultaneously transform into jackals. I take one last look at my father and mother as the golden doors fly open. Anput trots toward the portal, to the mundane world, and I follow. As we step into the darkness, intense memories flood my mind; the joy of bathing in Ra's sunlight, of wandering the deserts surrounding the pyramids and of helping others upon Earth.

As soulmates for eternity, Anput and I leave the Duat and go to our kas.

Chapter 22

I jolt awake to the sound of my alarm clock buzzing. I've fallen asleep reading *The Egyptian Book of the Dead* again. Yawning, I drop my book on the nightstand and turn off my alarm. It's still dark out, and I reflect on last night's delusion. It was so mild and only came to me while I was nearing sleep – I suspect it may be the last, as the night in the Duat has drawn to a close.

I get dressed and head to the garage. My car looks nice with its new paint job. I'm glad I steered away from a really ostentatious color. It's heartening to see the car's been restored. If it was left much longer, it wouldn't have been salvageable with all the rust it had.

I start the engine and give it a second to warm up before reversing out of the garage. I stop when I make it to the top of the driveway, taking a moment to look down at the town and city off in the distance – the horizon's a gradient of black and dark blue seamlessly blending together. I think back to the last moments I was with

Mom, how she praised Khepri, and I smile. Up in the sky, only the brightest stars are still visible, and I wonder if one of them is Mom, as an akh in the celestial sphere.

I carefully look both ways and turn toward Belinda's.

When I arrive, she's already waiting for me on the front steps.

"Mooorning."

I chuckle. "It's too early."

We make our way to the lookout, and once there, sit on a giant boulder. I wrap my arm around her waist, and she nestles her head on my shoulder. As we sit quietly, I reflect on the past six months.

On the edge of my mad existence, I found my true self. A self that is strong, a self that is not alone, a self I'm grateful to have found in time before it was too late. It's all so clear to me now, the demon within was never going to be slain by swords or daggers or javelins, it was only ever going to be defeated by the most ancient of human conditions: ties with my community and love for those whom which I call family.

With winter now behind us, I feel human once more. It's been a long time since I've been this happy; after suffering from depression for so long, and after walking through hell, I feel like a survivor. I'm determined now more than ever to make my time on Earth count.

The horizon slowly morphs into rich oranges and reds, and the darkness loses out to light. I picture Khepri leaving the Duat, traveling through the Gap of Bakhu before rising in the east. Just as I think this, Khepri peers over the mountains in the distance, blessing us with his light.

We watch as the giant sun-disk rises and fills the sky with light. The blinding orange light beams warmth down upon us and forms a full circle.

Praise to Khepri, O Great God of the east,

for you breathe new life into my ka,

for you breathe warmth into my ba,

for I am … reborn.

Made in the USA
Columbia, SC
04 July 2022

62782592R00200